Rag, Tag and Bobtail

and Other Magical Stories

Enid Blyton

Rag, Tag and Bobtail

and Other Magical Stories

Illustrated by Hannah George

MACMILLAN CHILDREN'S BOOKS

These stories first published 1950 by Macmillan & Co. Ltd in *Rag, Tag and Bobtail and other stories* and *The Three Naughty Children*

This collection published 2016 by Macmillan Children's Books
an imprint of Pan Macmillan
20 New Wharf Road, London N1 9RR
Associated companies throughout the world
www.panmacmillan.com

ISBN 978-1-5098-1084-0 (PB)
ISBN 978-1-5098-2744-2 (HB)

1 3 5 7 9 8 6 4 2

A CIP catalogue record for this book is available from
the British Library.

Printed and bound by CPI Group (UK) Ltd, Croydon CR0 4YY

Contents

Rag, Tag and Bobtail

Rag, Tag and Bobtail were three small pixies, all as mischievous as could be. They lived together in Windy Cottage and worked for old Lady Grumble, the wise woman on the hill.

Rag scrubbed the floors, Tag swept and Bobtail dusted. For this work Lady Grumble paid them sixpence a day each, which didn't buy them anything very grand to eat or to wear. But they were so quarrelsome that nobody else would give them work, and old Lady Grumble didn't mind how they quarrelled, for she was deaf and couldn't hear.

Rag and the others were half afraid of the wise woman, for she knew a great deal of magic. She knew how to make spells, and how to grant wishes, she knew how to turn people into frogs and how to change a beetle into a prince. She really was very clever indeed.

When she first had the three pixies to work for her she warned them on no account to touch any of her magic bottles or boxes.

'You don't know what may happen if you begin to meddle with magic you know nothing about,' she said. 'So keep your little fingers away from my magic cupboard, Rag, Tag and Bobtail.'

For a long time they did – and then one day Rag found a little yellow box on the floor.

'Look!' he cried, pointing with his scrubbing brush. 'There's a tiny yellow box. It must have fallen out of Lady Grumble's magic cupboard. One of you pick it up and look inside to see what there is in it.'

'Look inside it yourself!' cried Tag. 'Coward!'

'I'm *not* a coward!' cried Rag, and he boldly picked up the box. 'Ho, coward am I, Tag? Well, I've picked it up – and now *you* can open the box!'

And with that the rude pixie threw the box straight into Tag's surprised face. The box burst open and out fell a pile of purple sweets.

The pixies stared at them in astonishment, for they knew quite well what they were! They were wishing-sweets! Whoever swallowed one of those purple sweets and wished would have his wish come true.

'I say!' said Bobtail, looking down at the sweets. 'Shall we keep them and eat them?'

'No,' said Rag. 'Lady Grumble would find out and punish us.'

'We could wish her away to the moon!' cried Tag.

'No, let's go and tell her we found the box

of wishing-sweets and ask her to let us have one each,' said Tag. 'She will think we are very honest pixies, then, and will perhaps reward us for being good.'

So Tag picked up the sweets, put them back into the yellow box, and then all three of the pixies went to tell Lady Grumble. She was lying down in the back room of her cottage, thinking out a wonderful moonlight spell. They had to shout at her to make her hear what they had to say.

When she understood that they had found the sweets and were bringing them to her, she seemed pleased. But she shook her head when they asked her if she would let them have a sweet each.

'Wishes are only for sweet-natured people,' she said. 'Bad-tempered and quarrelsome creatures like you should never be allowed to have wishes. You only do harm.'

'Oh, please, please let us have a wish each,' said Rag. 'We won't quarrel, we won't be bad-tempered, we'll be good and kind. Really and truly.'

He had to shout it all over again before Lady Grumble heard what he said. She looked at him and shook her head doubtfully.

'Well, well,' she said, opening the box of sweets. 'I'll do as you say – but mind, pixies, if you are *not* kind and loving to one another, you will find that the wishes do you harm instead of good. So be careful!'

Joyfully the pixies popped a sweet into their mouths and thanked Lady Grumble. Then they ran to the kitchen to talk about their good fortune.

'Think of it!' said Rag, jumping up and down in delight. 'A wish for each of us! What shall we wish? Who will wish first?'

'Shall we wish to be very rich indeed?' said Tag.

'Or shall we wish never to work any more,' shouted Bobtail.

'What about wishing for a palace bigger than the King's?' said Rag. 'That *would* be exciting!'

'And a hundred servants!' cried Tag.

'And chocolate pudding and ice-cream for dinner every day!' said Bobtail, smacking his lips in delight. 'Ooh! How I wish we could have a great big ice-cream each now! I'm so hot and . . .'

He stopped – for before him on the table appeared three very large ice-creams, one strawberry, one vanilla and one chocolate!

Rag, Tag and Bobtail stared at them in the greatest dismay – and then Rag turned on Bobtail in rage.

'You silly, stupid, foolish, ridiculous pixie!' he cried, angrily. 'Look what you've wasted your wish on! Just look!'

'Yes, look!' shouted Tag. 'Three silly ice-creams, when we could have had sacks and sacks of gold! Oh, you fool!'

'Fool yourself!' cried Bobtail, in a rage too. 'I didn't think what I was saying, that's all! I just said it and they came, those three ice-creams!'

'Well you've wasted your wish nicely,' said Rag. 'Tag and I are not going to be so silly. We are going to wish for a big palace and lots of servants.'

'No, I'm not,' said Tag. 'I've thought of something else I'd rather have. I want a nice white horse to ride on. I've always wanted a white horse.'

'White horse!' cried Rag. 'You silly creature! Fancy wanting a white horse when you could have all the stables in the world! Why not wish for a *hundred* white horses if you want such a silly thing!'

'It's *not* a silly thing to want!' said Tag, fiercely. 'Mind what you're saying, Rag. And look out for those ice-creams, you silly pixie! You've knocked mine on to the floor! I shall have *yours*!'

He was just going to pick up Rag's ice-cream and eat it when that bad-tempered little pixie picked it up himself and threw it at the astonished Tag.

'There!' cried Rag, angrily. 'Have it if you like – and may it drip all down your neck till it makes you cough and sneeze without stopping!'

The ice-cream splashed into Tag's face, and began to drip down his neck. Tag tried to wipe it away but it wouldn't be wiped. It stuck there, dripping, dripping, dripping! The wish had come true!

'Oh, Rag, you wished a wish!' said Bobtail in horror. 'What a horrid wish! Poor Tag! He'll have ice-cream dripping down his neck for ever, and he'll cough and sneeze all day long!'

Sure enough Tag soon began to cough and sneeze without stopping, for the ice-cream was giving him a dreadful cold. Whatever was he to do?

'A-tishoo, a-tish-oo!' sneezed Tag, trying to find his handkerchief. 'Oh, you horrid thing, Rag! Look what you've done! Go and fetch Lady Grumble and ask her to take the nasty ice-cream away!'

So Rag fetched Lady Grumble and when she came and saw poor Tag with ice-cream running down his neck and heard him sneezing and coughing twenty times a minute, she *was* surprised.

'Please stop the ice-cream dripping down

Tag's neck,' begged Rag, nearly crying.

'But how did it get there?' asked Lady Grumble in great surprise.

'I wasted a wish and wished for ice-creams each,' said Bobtail, hanging his head.

'And I quarrelled with Tag and used my wish in wishing that his ice-cream should drip down his neck and make him cough and sneeze,' said Rag, very red indeed. 'And it's come true, though I didn't mean to wish it. Please, please, Lady Grumble, take away the spell.'

'But what about the third wish?' asked Lady Grumble. 'Hasn't Tag wished his wish yet?'

'Not yet,' said Rag.

'Well, why doesn't he use it to get rid of the ice-cream and to stop it dripping down his neck?' asked the wise woman.

'What, waste my wish in wishing a thing like that!' cried Tag, crossly. 'Not I! I'm keeping my wish for something grand. I'll be a rich man when Rag and Bobtail are poor! I'll show them what I can do with *my* wish! I'll punish Rag for doing this to me! A-tishoo! A-tishoo!'

'You are all three horrid, quarrelsome, unkind and selfish pixies!' said Lady Grumble, in disgust. 'I certainly shan't do anything to help you, Tag. If you want to get rid of that ice-cream, you can wish it away. But if you'd rather have it dripping down your neck all your life long, and be a rich man, well, you can choose!'

Tag stared at the wise woman in dismay.

'A-tishoo!' he said. 'Lady Grumble! Do, I beg of you, take away this spell and let me use my wish as I like! A-tishoo!'

But Lady Grumble seemed to become deaf again all of a sudden, and walked out of the room, laughing to herself. The three pixies looked at one another.

'A-tishoo!' wept poor Tag. 'I sh-shall have to use my w-w-wish to t-take this ice-c-cream, because it is so dreadfully cold and it's f-freezing my neck all the time it drips. Oh, dear, what a waste of a wish!'

'Never mind,' said Bobtail, feeling very sorry for his brother. 'Wish it, Tag. Quick, before you get a dreadful cold in your head!'

'I wish – a-tishoo – that this ice-cream would go away!' said poor Tag. At once the ice-cream disappeared, and Tag wiped away a few drops from his neck. He sneezed once more and then sat down on a stool.

The three pixies looked at one another. They could hear the wise woman chuckling away to herself in the back room, and they grew very red, for they guessed she was laughing at them.

'She said that bad-tempered people should never have wishes to wish,' said Bobtail, sadly. 'And it's true. Look at us! We could have been happy, rich and loved by everyone – and instead of that we are just three silly, poor, hard-working and quarrelsome little pixies.'

'We can't help being poor and hard-working,'

said Rag, 'but we *can* help being silly and quarrelsome. Let's cure our bad temper and be nice to one another. Then next time we have wishes to wish we shall use them properly and have everything we want!'

So they are trying very hard to be good and kind to one another, in case Lady Grumble one day *might* give them another chance. But I don't somehow think she will!

The Little Paper Boats

One night, when Paul and Mary were fast asleep, someone came knocking at their bedroom window.

'Tap!' went the noise. 'Tap-tap! Tap!'

Mary woke up first, and thought it was the wind blowing a branch against the window. Then she thought it wasn't, because it did sound so exactly like someone knocking. So she woke Paul up.

'Doesn't it sound as if someone is outside?' she whispered. 'Do you suppose it is a pixie?'

'Let's look!' said Paul and he jumped out of bed to see. The moon shone brightly outside – and what *do* you think he saw? Standing on the window-sill was a tiny creature dressed in silver, and she was tapping with her hand on the pane. 'Tap-tap! Tap!'

'It *is* a pixie or an elf!' cried Paul, in delight. He opened the window and the tiny creature climbed in.

'Oh, do forgive my waking you,' she said. 'But a dreadful thing has happened.'

'What?' cried both children.

'Well, you know the stream that runs to the bottom of your garden?' said the pixie. 'We were going to meet the Fairy Queen on the opposite side tonight, because she is going to hold a meeting there – and we had our pixie ship all ready to take us across. But a big wind blew suddenly and broke the rope that tied our ship to the shore. So now we can't get across because the ship has floated away, and we *are* so upset.'

'Oh, what a pity!' said Mary. 'Can we help you?'

'That's what I came to ask you,' said the pixie. 'Could you lend us a toy boat to sail across in?'

'We did have one,' said Paul, 'but it's broken. Its sail is gone, and it floats all on one side. I'm afraid it wouldn't be a bit of use to you.'

'Oh dear!' said the pixie, looking ready to burst into tears. 'Isn't that too bad? We felt quite sure you would have one. Have you anything else that would do?'

'No, I'm afraid not,' said Paul, trying to think of something. 'We've no raft, and not even a little penny rowing-boat. I *am* sorry!'

'Well, never mind,' said the pixie, climbing out to the window-sill. 'We shall just have to stay on this side of the stream and hope that the Queen will not be too cross with us. We have no wings, you see, or we could fly across.'

Mary suddenly clapped her hands. 'I know!'

she cried. 'I know! What about some paper boats, pixie? Paul and I can make nice paper boats that will float on the water. They don't last very long but they would take you across the stream all right, I'm sure. Shall we make you some?'

'Oh, will you?' asked the pixie, in delight. 'That *is* kind of you! Thank you so much!'

'That's a good idea of yours, Mary,' said Paul. 'Quick, let's put on our dressing-gowns and go down to the stream with the pixie. We can take a newspaper with us and make as many boats as they like.'

So they put on their dressing-gowns, took an old newspaper from the cupboard, and then ran downstairs and out into the garden. The pixie met them there and they all three went down to the little stream that ran at the foot of the garden.

What a sight the two children saw! The moon shone brightly down on a crowd of little silvery creatures, dressed in misty gowns. They had tiny pointed faces and little high voices like swallows twittering. They were astonished to see the children and ran helter-skelter to hide. But the pixie that came with Paul and Mary called them back.

'It's quite safe,' she cried. 'These children are going to help us. They will make us some boats.'

'A small boat will take one or two of you,'

said Paul. 'We'll make some of all sizes – and then some of you can go in crowds and some can go in twos and threes, just as you like.'

He and Mary began to tear the paper into oblongs, and then, very quickly, they folded their paper into this shape and that, until at last there came a little paper boat. The pixies watched them in delight. They had never seen such a thing before.

Paul and Mary soon put two boats on the water, and two or three pixies clambered in. The boat went rocking up and down on the stream, and the pixies guided it towards the opposite bank. They screamed with delight as it went, and all the pixies left on shore begged Paul and Mary to hurry up and make some more boats for them. Very soon there was a whole fleet of the little paper boats on the stream and the pixies sprang into them in joy. Across to the opposite shore they sailed one by one and landed safely on the opposite side.

The last pixie left was the one who had tapped on the bedroom window. Mary made her a dear little boat for herself and the pixie stepped into it.

'Good-bye,' she said. 'Don't wait here any longer, in case you catch cold. It's been so kind of you to help us. If you find our ship you may keep it for your own. It's a dear little ship, and we'd like you to have it.'

The children waved good-bye and then went indoors to bed, talking excitedly of all that had happened. They thought that they were much too excited to go to sleep, but it wasn't long before they were dreaming, their heads cuddled into their pillows.

The next day they were quite certain they had dreamt it all, and they were surprised to find that they had both had the same dream – but they really didn't think they *could* have seen pixies in the night. It didn't seem real in the morning.

But what do you think they found later on in the day, when they went for a walk down by their stream? The little ship belonging to the pixies! There it was, caught in some rushes, a little silver-sailed ship with the name 'Silver Pixie' on its hull! Then they knew that their dream was true, and in great delight they rushed home to show their mother what they had found.

They keep the ship on the nursery mantelpiece because it is so pretty – and there it is to this day, a little glittering, silver ship! It sails beautifully, and you should see all the children stare when Paul and Mary take it down to the pond to sail!

I'd love to see it, wouldn't you?

The Cat and the Wishing-Well

There was once a little boy who was most unkind to animals. He threw stones at birds, he chased dogs and he caught cats and tied tin cans to their tails. So you can guess that all the animals and birds around his home feared him and hated him.

His mother was angry with him.

'One day, Tim,' she said, 'you will be very sorry for your horrid mischief. How would *you* like to be chased, or have tin-cans tied to you?'

'Pooh!' said Tim. 'I shouldn't mind at all!'

Now it happened that the very next day Tim chased the next-door cat and frightened the poor creature so much that it fell down the well at the bottom of the garden. Tim roared with laughter, but he didn't go to help the cat. No, he left the poor thing to get out as best it could.

The cat swam to the side of the well, and held on to the loose bricks with its claws. 'How I wish that I could do to Tim all the things he does to me and to the dogs and birds!' thought the cat.

The animal did not know that the well was a wishing-well! Whatever you wished when drawing water from the well, came true – and if anyone wished a wish right inside the well, the wish came true at once.

And so the cat's wish came true! As soon as someone came to draw water, the cat climbed into the bucket and was hauled safely to the top of the well, wet and shivering. She felt strange, because she was full of magic. She hopped on

23

to the brick wall round the well and began to lick herself.

Tim was playing in the garden next door. He took up a stone and threw it at a sparrow. The cat lifted her head, and, much surprised at herself, said in a loud voice: 'Birds, throw stones at Tim!'

At once all the sparrows, thrushes, blackbirds, robins and starlings picked up stones in their beaks and dropped them on Tim! He was frightened and astonished to find big and little stones dropping on his bare head.

He ran away – and the cat saw him and cried out: 'Dogs! Chase this boy as he has

so many times chased you!'

At once all the dogs around jumped up and ran after Tim. He tore away, yelling with fear, but nobody came to his help. The dogs rushed after him, and one of them nipped his fat leg. Another jumped and bit his thumb. This was a dog that Tim had beaten with a stick and he was glad to punish the horrid little boy.

'Now, cats, it's your turn!' cried the cat on the well. 'Find some old tin cans on the rubbish-heap and tie them to his coat! Then make him run and see how he likes the horrible clanking noise behind him!'

At once about eight cats of all sizes and colours rushed to the rubbish-heap and found some old tins. They carried them to the corner where the dogs were snarling at Tim and between them they fastened the tins by string to the boy's coat. Then the dogs set him running again, and when poor Tim heard the awful clinking-clanking noise behind him, he was more frightened than ever, and tore on faster and faster.

The cans flew off, one after another, as they banged against the road. But Tim still ran, frightened out of his life, chased by half the dogs and cats in the town. At last he stumbled up to the old well and leaned against it, panting.

'Let's push him in!' cried the first cat. 'He pushed *me* in! Let's push *him* in!'

'No, no!' begged Tim, frightened. 'No, please, please don't. I've learnt my lesson. I know what it is to be hurt and frightened. I didn't know before. I'll never, never throw stones again or chase you or be unkind. I'll always be good and careful with animals.'

'Well,' said a little brown dog to the cat, 'shall we let him? Once he gave me a drink of water when I was thirsty – so for the sake of that one kind deed, shall we let him go?'

'Very well,' said the cat, licking herself, 'for the sake of that one kind deed. It's a good thing he did *one* kind act in his life!'

'I'll do heaps more now!' promised Tim, sobbing. 'I'd no idea how horrid I'd been to you. I didn't think. But I'm going to be different now. Let me lie down here in the sunshine and rest. My legs are so tired and I am full of bumps where the stones hit me.'

So the animals allowed him to lie down and fall asleep. The birds flew back to the trees and forgot about him. The dogs went back to their kennels, yawning. The cats lay down in the sun and slept. Only the cat that had fallen down the well was awake – but she soon settled down in the sun and fell asleep too, dreaming with delight of how she had punished that horrid boy, Tim.

When she awoke the magic had gone out of her. She was just an ordinary cat, and she had forgotten all about her wish that had come true. Tim woke up too – but he hadn't forgotten. He sat up and wondered if he had dreamt it all.

But there were bumps and bruises on his head and arms, so he thought it must really have happened.

He went back home, thinking hard. He saw a cat on a wall, and to that animal's great surprise he stroked it! He met a dog and patted it! The dog was astonished, and licked Tim's hand. Tim was pleased to feel its little pink tongue.

'I've learnt my lesson,' he thought. 'Oh dear, what a dreadful dream that was! Or was it a dream? I really don't know!'

Tim's mother couldn't think what had happened to Tim after that. He put crumbs out for the birds. He bought a little tin trough and kept it full of water for dogs to drink in the hot weather. He brought home a stray cat that somebody had left behind and begged his mother to keep it.

'Well, you're a different boy, Tim!' said his mother, pleased. 'Goodness knows what's happened to you! Perhaps the dogs and cats treated you as you used to treat them and taught you a lesson. Something's changed you, anyway!'

Tim didn't tell his mother what had happened – he was much too ashamed – but he told me his story to tell to you, and that's how I know all about it. Wasn't it a strange thing to happen?

The Surprising Hoop-Sticks

Once upon a time there were two little gnomes called Tups and Twinkle. They were very fond of all kinds of toys, and they had beautiful sailing-ships, fine spinning-tops, big kites and all sorts of things.

They were very pleased with themselves one day because they had made two hoops. You should have seen those hoops! They were as big as the gnomes themselves and they were painted all sorts of colours. Tied to the inside edge of the hoops were tiny bells that rang when the hoops were bowled along.

All the gnomes were busy making hoops for themselves as soon as they saw those of Tups and Twinkle. What a tinkling and jingling there was in Heigho Village when all the hoops were set rolling!

'Let's have a Grand Hoop-Race,' said Tups one day to the others. 'That would be fun. We could start at one end of the village and finish up at the other.'

'That's a good idea,' said all the gnomes. So they made plans for a great hoop-race, and the prize was to be three gold pennies to spend at the cake-shop and at the sweet-shop.

Tups and Twinkle practised bowling their hoops every morning and evening, for they meant to win the prize.

'We could have peppermints from the sweet-shop and currant buns from the cake-shop every day for a year if we won the prize,' said Tups.

'I wish we could be quite sure of winning it,'

said Twinkle. 'I wish we could get some hoop-sticks that would bowl our hoops faster than anyone else's.'

Twinkle looked at Tups and Tups looked at Twinkle. Then they sat down and thought hard, and it wasn't long before Tups had a bright idea.

'I say, Twinkle!' he said. 'I know what we'll do. We'll go to Wizard Too-Wise's garden after supper tonight, when it's dark, and we'll cut ourselves two nice strong hoop-sticks from the wishing-tree in his front garden. Then we'll use them for our hoops on the race day and we'll be sure to win the prize!'

So that night when it was dark the two naughty gnomes went along to Wizard Too-Wise's house. They knew exactly where the wishing-tree was, and it didn't take them long to cut themselves two fine sticks from it. Then off they went – but the gate creaked as they went out and the wizard heard it.

'Robbers!' he cried, looking out of the window.
'Thieves! Burglars! May whatever you steal
bring you back to me to punish!'

'Ooh!' said Tups and Twinkle, running away
as fast as they could. 'We were nearly caught!'

They hadn't heard what the wizard said,
and they would have been very much worried if
they had; for his magic was powerful and never
failed. They soon forgot their fright and put
away their new hoop-sticks in the cupboard to

wait for the great hoop-race.

The day came at last, and proudly the two little gnomes took their hoops to the edge of the village to join all the others. What a number of hoops there were! Green ones, blue ones, red, yellow, purple and orange ones, and some like Tups's and Twinkle's, all colours of the rainbow with little bells inside.

The two gnomes had their new hoop-sticks from the wizard's wishing-tree. They hadn't used them yet. They were busy wishing that their hoop-sticks should make their hoops go faster than any other gnome's so that they would be sure to win the prize.

Off they all went. Tap-tap-tap went the hoop-sticks on the rolling hoops. Down the winding village street ran a score of panting gnomes with their bright hoops, and far in front of everyone were Tups and Twinkle, their hoops tinkling merrily as they ran.

'We shall win!' shouted Tups to Twinkle.

'Aren't our new sticks wonderful? They make our hoops go like the wind!'

But dear me, what a peculiar thing happened when the race was over! Tups and Twinkle won easily, and just as the prize was being given to them, something curious happened. Their feet and hands bent over and joined one another, and in a trice they were rolling over and over just like hoops! They were like big wheels rolling along – and oh, dear me, what was this that the hoop-sticks were doing?

The sticks leapt up in the air and began to hit the rolling, bowling gnomes, driving them along fast! Smack! Smack! Smack! How those sticks hurt when they hit the rolling gnomes! Tups and Twinkle shouted in pain and fright, and all the other gnomes looked on in amazement.

Back up the village street went the bowling gnomes, rolling along merrily in the dust, the two magic hoop-sticks hitting them hard all the time. At last they came to Wizard Too-Wise's house and the gnomes rolled in at the gate, the hoop-sticks behind them.

Wizard Too-Wise was watering his wishing-tree and when he saw the two gnomes coming in at his gate, rolling up his garden path, he set down his can and roared till the tears ran down his cheeks. The gnomes had never seen him laugh so much before.

'So here are the thieves come back to me!' he said at last. 'Dear, dear, dear, what a very comical sight! So you thought you would get magic hoop-sticks, did you, and win the prize by cheating? Well, well, this is a very good punishment for you. Would you like to keep your magic hoop-sticks, Tups and Twinkle? They will be very pleased to bowl you anywhere you want to go.'

'Oh no, no,' said the gnomes, weeping bitterly. 'Take them away, and please, please, forgive us. We were very wrong. We will never cheat again. We might have won the prize if we had used our own hoop-sticks, but now we have lost it, and have been bowled all round the village for everyone to see. We are very bruised and ashamed. Please forgive us and let us go.'

The wizard said a few words and the hoop-sticks flew back to the wishing-tree and grew there again as branches. The gnomes found themselves able to stand upright, and, very red in the face, they walked back home, dusty, dirty and bruised.

'We will never, never cheat again in anything we do,' they said solemnly to one another.

And you may be quite sure they never, never did!

The Little Pinching Girl

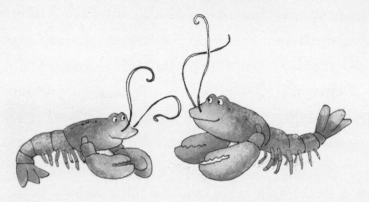

Nobody liked Elsie, because she was always pinching people. Wasn't it horrid of her? At school she pinched the little boy who sat next to her and made him cry out. At home she pinched her little sister and the twins next door. When she went out to play she pinched the children near to her, and they didn't like it at all.

Elsie's mother was cross with her.

'Why don't you stop pinching people?' she said. 'They don't like it, because it hurts them. You are a very unkind child, Elsie, to pinch others. It is a stupid habit and you must stop it, or you will be very sorry.'

But Elsie didn't stop. She pinched Joan, and she pinched Tom. She pinched Alan, and she pinched Willie – but she didn't pinch Big Mary, because Big Mary could slap very hard. She really was a very horrid little girl.

And then one day something happened. She went down to the seaside for her Sunday School treat. It was great fun, because all the children went in motor-coaches, and they were very much excited about it. Elsie was so excited that she pinched children all the way, so that nobody wanted to sit next to her. But somebody had to, of course, so Elsie always had some poor child to pinch.

When they arrived at the seaside they all went to the sands and sat down to eat their dinner. Elsie was hungry and she soon finished hers. Afterwards she felt sleepy and she lay down by a big sand-castle and shut her eyes.

She hadn't shut them for more than a moment when she heard voices not far from her.

'This must be our dear little friend,' said one of the voices. 'How nice it is to see her!'

'Yes, this is Elsie,' said another voice. 'We must shake hands with her and tell her how very pleased we are to see her.'

Elsie opened her eyes and sat up with a jerk. Who was talking?

She saw a very strange sight. Two large

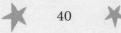

lobsters were sitting against the sand-castle, looking at her with broad smiles on their funny faces. She stared at them in astonishment.

'Oh, good morning, Elsie,' said one of the lobsters, holding out a great pincer-paw to the surprised little girl. 'We are *so* pleased to see you. We know you are a great friend of ours.'

Elsie put out her hand to shake the lobster's claw – and how she shouted and yelled! The lobster was pinching her fingers in its trap-like claw, and wouldn't let go.

'Let go!' shouted Elsie, with tears in her eyes. 'Oh, you horrid creature, you're hurting me!'

'But I'm only pinching you,' said the lobster in surprise. 'You are very fond of pinching, aren't you? That is why we are so pleased to welcome you here as our dear little friend. We are fond of pinching too.'

'Will you let my hand go?' wept Elsie, trying to take her hand away from the lobster's great claw. At last he let it go, and the little girl nursed her pinched hand and glared angrily at the big lobster. The other lobster leaned forward and held *his* claw to shake hands. But Elsie wouldn't touch it.

'No, you horrid creature,' she said. 'I'm not going to have my hand pinched again!'

'How impolite you are not to shake hands with me!' said the lobster, shocked. He came closer to Elsie and took hold of her arm. Dear me, how he pinched with his big claws! Elsie screamed and tried to shake off his claw, but she couldn't.

'What's the matter, now, what's the matter?' asked the lobster, surprised. 'You're a pincher, aren't you? You love pinching, I know, so why do you make such a fuss when you meet two nice pinchers like ourselves? We thought you would be very pleased to see us.'

'Well, I'm not, then,' said Elsie, wishing with all her heart that she had never pinched anyone in her life.

'Perhaps she will be better pleased to meet our cousins the crabs,' said the first lobster. 'Here they come.'

Elsie saw about a dozen crabs hurrying up the beach, some large and some small, all waving their pincer-like claws to her as they came scuttling up sideways.

They crowded round her and soon began to nip her bare legs and toes.

'Ooh!' cried Elsie, trying to get her legs safely under her. 'Stop nipping me, you horrid little things!'

The crabs looked at her in astonishment.

'Aren't you a pincher too?' they asked. 'We thought you were the little girl who loves pinching.'

'Well, I don't like *being* pinched,' wept Elsie. 'Do go away.'

'Why don't you pinch *us*?' said the crabs. 'You can pinch us back, you know. We expect it.'

Elsie tried to pinch a crab very hard. But it

43

had a thick shell and it didn't mind a bit. It caught hold of her thumb and nipped it.

'This is a fine game!' cried the crabs and lobsters excitedly. 'Come on, Elsie – you try to pinch us, and we'll try to pinch you!'

But it wasn't a fair game, because Elsie's hands and legs were soft and it hurt her to be pinched. The crabs and lobsters all wore hard shells and they couldn't be pinched. Elsie kicked at them and tried to knock them away.

'Don't you like us?' said the big lobsters sadly. 'We did so look forward to your coming to the seaside. We thought it would be so nice to welcome another member of the pinching family. Do play with us, Elsie. You pinch other children hundreds of times a day – why can't you play at pinching with us?'

'I'm never never going to pinch anyone again,' wept Elsie. 'I didn't know it could be so horrid. I don't belong to your nasty pinching family. I'm going to be a nice kind little girl who doesn't pinch or slap or pull hair. I'm ashamed of myself for being like crabs and lobsters, so there!'

When the crabs and lobsters heard her saying this they all cried out in horror and scuttled down the shore to the sea as fast as ever they could.

'She's not a friend of ours!' they shouted. 'She isn't a pincher any more!'

Elsie wiped her eyes with her handkerchief and looked round. Someone was coming towards her. It was her Sunday School teacher.

'Come along and play, Elsie!' she cried. 'Have you been asleep?'

'No,' said Elsie, scrambling to her feet. 'But I've had a very nasty adventure. Do you know, some crabs and lobsters came and told me I belonged to their nasty pinching family, and they wanted me to play pinching each other with them. And I told them I'm never going to pinch anyone again.'

'I'm very glad,' said her teacher. 'People will like you much better if you are kind and gentle.'

Elsie has never pinched anyone from that day – and the other children don't mind sitting next to her now. I'm glad *I* don't pinch people, aren't you? I wouldn't like to play with crabs and lobsters at all!

The Tale of Flop and Whiskers

Flop and Whiskers were two white rabbits belonging to Malcolm and Jean. They had fine whiskers, little black bobtails and big floppy ears. Malcolm and Jean were very fond of them and looked after them well.

Flop and Whiskers lived happily enough in a big cage. They were friendly with one another, but sometimes they found things dull.

'Oh, if only something exciting would happen!' Flop would sigh.

'Yes, something that we could remember and

talk about for weeks and weeks,' said Whiskers. 'But nothing ever happens to pet rabbits. They just live in a cage and eat and sleep. That's all.'

But one night something *did* happen! Flop and Whiskers heard a noise in the garden, and looked out of their cage. It was bright moonlight and coming down the garden path was a long procession of fairies. In their midst was a snow-white carriage with gold handles and gold wheels. It was drawn by six coal-black rabbits.

'Just look at that!' cried Flop, excitedly. 'It must be a fairy princess of some kind. Oh, don't I wish I was one of those rabbits pulling her carriage! Wouldn't I feel grand!'

'Isn't it beautiful?' said Whiskers, his little nose pressed against the wires of the cage.

The procession came down the path and passed by the rabbits' cage. They were so excited. They could see a golden-haired princess in the snow-white carriage and just as she passed their cage she leaned out and blew a kiss to them. Flop scraped at the wire of the cage, trying her hardest to get out and run after the procession – but it was no use, the wire was too strong.

'Look!' suddenly cried Whiskers. 'The procession has stopped. What has happened?'

'One of the coal-black rabbits has gone lame,' said Flop. 'See, its foot is limping.'

What a to-do there was! All the fairies gathered round the limping rabbit, who shook his head dolefully and held up his foot in pain.

The princess leaned out of her carriage and pointed to the rabbit-hutch she had just passed. She called out something in her high little voice.

'I say, Flop, I believe the princess is saying that one of us could draw her carriage instead of the lame rabbit!' said Whiskers, in excitement. 'Oh, I wonder which of us will be chosen.'

The little fairies came running back to the

cage and climbed up to the wire.

'Will you come and draw our princess's carriage just for tonight?' they cried. 'One of our rabbits has hurt its foot.'

'Oh yes!' squeaked the two white rabbits in delight. 'But which of us do you want?'

'Both of you, please,' said the fairies. 'You see, the rabbits have to go in pairs, and we couldn't make one of the pairs a black rabbit and a white one. We shall set free the hurt rabbit and his companion, so that we can have two white rabbits instead. So will you both come? You shall be brought back before sunrise.'

Flop and Whiskers joyfully told the fairies how to open their cage and then they jumped out in delight. In a trice they were harnessed with the other rabbits, and the two black ones, whose place they were taking, hopped away into the hedges. The fairies cried out in delight to see the two beautiful white rabbits among the coal-black ones.

They made such a noise that they woke up Malcolm and Jean. The children jumped out of bed and went to their bedroom window, looking out into the moonlight.

They saw the fairy procession going along down the garden path and they stared in astonishment.

'Jean!' said Malcolm, 'look at those two white rabbits with black tails, drawing the carriage along with the four black rabbits. Don't they look like Flop and Whiskers?'

'Yes, they do,' said Jean. 'And oh, look! Malcolm, their cage door is open. I can see it quite plainly in the moonlight.'

The children ran downstairs to see the procession, but it had passed by before they were in the garden. So they went to see if the rabbit-cage was open – and it was.

'Oh dear, I *shall* be sorry not to have dear old Flop and Whiskers,' said Jean, almost crying. 'They were so sweet. I don't think it was very kind of the fairies to take them away from us.'

But the next morning the cage door was fast shut and the two white rabbits were safely back in their hutch once more! When Malcolm and Jean went to peep, they found both rabbits fast asleep in the hay, and they didn't even wake when the children put some fresh lettuce in for them.

'Goodness, aren't they tired!' said Jean. 'I expect they walked for miles last night, dragging that lovely carriage behind them. I do wonder where they went.'

Where *did* they go? Well, they went to a party! The Prince of Derry-Down Palace was just twenty-one and he had sent out invitations to his birthday party – and, of course, the golden-haired princess had one of the beautiful invitation cards too.

Her name was Fenella, and she loved parties. She had only just grown up, so she hadn't been to many big parties. She had a new dress and new silver shoes made, and she looked very lovely in them.

'I will lend you my second-best coach, the white one with gold wheels,' said her father, the King. 'And you shall have either my six well-matched coal-black rabbits to draw it, or my six white cats with pink eyes.'

The princess chose the rabbits, and they were the very ones that the two children had seen in the night. The two white rabbits, Flop and Whiskers, watched the two black ones whose place they took, run into the hedge, and then off they went with the other four.

'I hope we keep up all right,' panted Flop. 'We aren't very used to galloping, we've been so used to sitting in our cage.'

But they galloped along just as fast as the black rabbits, and the princess was very pleased. 'They shall go to the Rabbits' Party,' she said to the fairies with her. 'They deserve it.'

The Prince was giving a party for his friends and the rabbits he sometimes rode were giving a party for the six rabbits who drew the princess's coach – so you can imagine the delight of Flop and Whiskers when four fine rabbits, with bows round their necks, made them welcome to their own little party in the grounds of the palace!

They were given blue bows to wear, and sat down at little tables with dishes of delicious looking food.

'Look, Flop,' said Whiskers. 'Carrot Sandwiches!'

'And see – that's Cabbage Pie!' said Flop. 'And here's Turnip Cake. And what's this – Lettuce Biscuits! What a wonderful meal!'

It certainly was – and afterwards the ten rabbits had a little dance of their own. Flop and Whiskers were very sorry when it was all over. They pulled the princess's carriage home for her – and then they ran back to their cage and curled up to go to sleep, tired out!

Flop and Whiskers longed to tell the children all about their adventures, but they couldn't. When they woke up they looked at one another in delight, and Flop said: 'Did we dream it, Whiskers, or was it true?'

'Quite true,' said Whiskers. 'We've had an adventure at last, Flop. We can talk about it for weeks and weeks, and we'll never feel dull again.'

So they talk about it all day long – and I wish I could listen to them, don't you?

Peter's Horrid Afternoon

Peter wanted a bicycle. He wanted one very badly indeed, so badly that he made up his mind to be a very good, kind, unselfish boy for weeks. Then he hoped that his mother would buy him a bicycle.

It wasn't very difficult for Peter to be kind and unselfish, for he was a good-hearted boy and always willing to do a good turn for anyone. His mother didn't really notice very much difference, for Peter was always good to her. But Peter was hoping and hoping that she would notice how hard he was trying to be good so that she would give him a reward.

One day, after he had been trying hard for about four weeks, he asked his mother a question.

'Do you think I deserve a bicycle, Mother?' he asked.

'Deserve a bicycle!' said his mother in surprise. 'What for?'

'Well, haven't I been good as can be all these weeks?' said Peter. 'I thought you would be sure to notice. Didn't you?'

'Well, no, I didn't,' said his mother. She was just about to say that Peter was *always* a kind-hearted boy, but he didn't give her time. He went very red and looked quite cross and upset.

'Well, really, Mother!' he said, 'I don't see any use in my trying so hard if nobody is going to notice. You did once say that if I were a very specially good boy you might think of buying me a bicycle, and now I expect you've forgotten all about it! It's no use being kind! It's no use being good! I just won't be any more!'

Peter's mother was so astonished that she couldn't say a word. Peter walked out of the room and went into the garden. He felt very cross and disappointed. It was too bad to have tried so hard for so long and then to be told that his mother hadn't even noticed he was any better. He didn't guess it was because he was always such a kindly boy that his mother hadn't noticed anything different about him.

'I'll go for a walk all by myself,' thought Peter, half-sulky with his disappointment. 'I'll go up on the common, past the police-station and down by the sweet-shop. And I won't do a kind deed to anyone, and I won't smile or say good afternoon. I'll just be simply horrid and see if anyone notices *that*!'

So, much to everyone's surprise, Peter went frowning through the village and didn't raise his cap to anyone or say good afternoon. He saw old

Mrs Harrison coming and because he didn't want to shake hands with her and be his usual kind self he turned his back on her and pretended to read a notice outside the police-station.

It was quite an interesting notice, all about a robbery that had taken place in a big house not far away. Peter read about the things that had been stolen, and at the end it said that it was believed that the thieves had hidden the stolen things somewhere, and anyone finding them must report to the police.

'I wish *I* could find them!' thought Peter. 'It would be exciting. I'd like that. I'll look under the bushes on the common as I pass them. You never know what might happen!'

So he went on his way feeling a little happier. But when he passed Harry Brown, waving a brand-new kite to show him, he remembered that he was being horrid that afternoon and he scowled and looked away. Harry was so surprised.

He was soon up on the common. A little girl threw a ball near to him and asked him to throw it back – but Peter took no notice at all and stalked on, his hands in his pockets. He WAS NOT going to be kind. It didn't pay. Nobody noticed. He might as well be horrid! Wasn't he being silly?

He passed by some goats and a little goat kid tied to a post. The rope had got wound round one of its legs and Peter saw it. He was just going to run over and free it when he remembered that he was being horrid. No, he must leave the kid as it was. On he went, scowling all round, looking under the bushes as he passed. But there was no sack of stolen things anywhere. Only dead leaves lay under the bushes.

Then he suddenly heard the sound of someone crying. He looked about and saw Pam, a little girl he knew. She was weeping bitterly, and when she saw him she ran to him.

'Oh, Peter, Peter!' she cried. 'Will you help

me? I've dropped my doll down this big hole here, and I can't get it back.'

Peter badly wanted to help her, but he remembered that he was being horrid.

'I'm sorry,' he said, 'I'm not doing any kind deeds today. I can't get your doll.'

'Oh, Peter, please, please do!' sobbed Pam. 'I do want her so. I can't leave her there. I'll have to climb down myself and I'm afraid.'

Peter looked at the little girl and then he suddenly thought it was a nasty thing to be horrid to people. He didn't care whether he had a reward or not – he was going to be good and kind whatever happened! He wanted to be. It didn't matter if he had a bicycle or anything else for being good – he could be kindly without that. How could he let Pam climb down that big crack in the earth and get her doll? She might break her leg!

He went to the hole where she said her doll had fallen. There was a great crack in the common just there and a large and jagged hole ran down into the earth. Bushes grew here and there in the crack, which was steep and dangerous. But Peter wanted to help Pam so he began to climb down.

He could see the doll's blue dress not very far down and he soon reached it – and then, just as he was about to climb up again, he caught sight of something else poked into a hole nearby. It looked like an old sack! Peter pulled at it and it came away from its hiding-place. He slid down a little further and opened the sack. Inside were all the things that had been stolen by the thieves when they had robbed the big house!

Peter felt so excited that he could hardly speak. At last he found his tongue. 'Pam!' he cried. 'Isn't it exciting! I believe I've found all the things those robbers stole the other night! Quick! We'll go and tell the police where they are. The sack is too heavy for me to pull up.'

He climbed out of the crack and he and Pam

set off as fast as they could run to the police-station. They told a policeman what they had found, and very soon all three were going back to the hole again – and sure enough the sack of stolen goods was there! The policeman was pleased, and took it away on his back. Pam was excited too, and as for Peter, he could hardly go home fast enough, he was so eager to tell his mother all about it.

All the stolen goods were sent back to the owner, and when he heard who had found them, he called at Peter's house to give him a reward.

'I offered five pounds to anyone who could tell me where my goods were hidden by the thieves,' he said to Peter's mother. 'Would Peter like the money, do you think, or would he rather have a present?'

'He is at school just now,' said his mother, 'but if you would like to give him a present, I know what he would like – a bicycle!'

'He shall have one!' said the man at once. 'I'll buy him one today.' And that afternoon what should Peter see waiting for him in the garden but the brightest, newest, finest bicycle he had ever imagined! He was simply delighted. Then he went rather red and looked at his mother.

'You know, Mother,' he said, 'I was being very silly and horrid that afternoon. I just wouldn't be kind or polite to anyone – but when I saw

Pam so miserable I *had* to help her – and that's how I found the stolen goods.'

'Ah, Peter, you see you were rewarded for your kindness after all,' said his mother smiling. 'It is always best to be kind, for somehow and some time kindness brings its own reward – though you don't need to think about that. Now go and ride your bicycle.'

'I shall give Pam the first ride!' said Peter. 'If she hadn't dropped her doll down that hole I would never have found the sack! So she deserves the first ride!'

Off he went – and isn't he proud of that bright new bicycle! I would be too, wouldn't you?

The Palace of Bricks

Donald and Mary had a big box of bricks between them. The bricks were all colours, and there were so many that the two children could build really big houses, castles and palaces.

One sunny day Mummy said they could take their bricks out into the garden and build there. She gave them a big flat piece of cardboard to build on, and Mary carried that out, whilst Donald took the box of bricks.

'Let's build a palace today,' said Donald. 'We've got all afternoon to build it. There's a fine palace in the book that goes with the bricks – look! It shows you just what bricks to use, and how to make the towers and pinnacles on top of the palace.'

So they began. It was very difficult, but perfectly lovely to do. They had to find all the right bricks, and put them in just the right places. The palace began to grow and when Mummy came out to look, she thought it was grand!

'It's fit for a Princess,' she said. 'It really is.'

They finished it just after tea. It stood out there in the garden, with all its little towers rising gracefully, the prettiest palace you would imagine!

Just as they had finished it Mummy called them.

'Donald! Mary! Here is Peter come to ask you to go and try his new see-saw!'

Donald and Mary left their palace of bricks and rushed to the front garden, where Peter stood waiting.

'Are you coming?' he asked. 'I've made a fine new see-saw out of a tree-trunk and a big plank.'

Off they all rushed and that was the last that Donald and Mary remembered of their palace before they went to bed that night! They had a fine time with Peter's see-saw and got back home so late that Mummy bundled them into bed at once. And nobody thought of the bricks left out-of-doors!

Now it began to rain heavily after the children were in bed, but they were asleep and didn't know. Outside in the darkness the palace of bricks stood, getting wetter and wetter. Soon, down the garden there shone many little lanterns, and the sound of high voices could be heard. The little sparrows roosting in the trees heard them and whispered to one another: 'It's the pixie-folk! They were going to have a party tonight! What a pity the rain will spoil it!'

It *did* spoil the party! The pixies were terribly

upset, especially as it was a birthday party for the little Princess Peronel.

'Whatever shall we do?' they cried, as they swung their lanterns here and there. 'The grass is much too wet to dance on, and all our cakes and jellies will be spoilt!'

'What's this?' suddenly cried a small pixie in yellow, running up to the palace of bricks. 'I say! Look at this! It's a beautiful palace! Why, it's just the thing to have the party in!'

All the pixies crowded round to see the palace. They were delighted with it. They ran inside the door and looked round the big rooms.

'They're quite dry!' they cried. 'The palace has a fine roof, and not a drop of rain is leaking through! Those children must have built it. Let's use it for our party!'

'Let's!' cried the Princess Peronel, peeping in too. 'I'd love to have a party here. Fetch the tables and the stools, and we'll soon have a fine time!'

It wasn't long before the palace was hung with shining lanterns, and set with little golden tables and stools. On the tables were all kinds of cakes, jellies and trifles, with little blue jugs of honey-lemonade to drink. The cardboard floor was soon polished up and the band took their places to play merry dance-tunes.

You should have seen inside that palace! It was perfectly lovely! The pixies were dancing together, talking at the tops of their little voices, and the Princess Peronel was sitting on a golden chair watching everyone with a happy smile on her face. The little lanterns shone brightly down, and nobody would ever have guessed that the palace was only built of toy bricks, and hadn't been made till that very afternoon.

Now the rain went on pouring down all night, and it pattered so hard against the children's window that at last it woke Donald and he sat up in bed. Then he suddenly remembered that they had left their bricks outside.

'Mary!' he said. 'Wake up! I say, aren't we silly, we've left that brick palace out-of-doors, and it's pouring with rain! It will all be spoilt in the morning, and Mummy will be so cross with us.'

'Oh dear!' said Mary, sitting up. 'Well, I know, Donald! Let's put on our dressing-gowns, with our mackintoshes over them, and our Wellington boots, and go out and get the bricks. It will be quite an adventure!'

So they quickly put on their dressing-gowns and their mackintoshes, and out they went into the dark garden. But when they came near the palace of bricks they stopped in the greatest astonishment.

'There are people inside!' whispered Mary. 'Look! It's all hung with lanterns! And there's a band playing!'

They stooped down and peeped into their palace. What an exciting sight they saw! They could hardly believe their eyes.

'Pixies!' said Donald. 'Pixies! Well, fancy that! We've always wanted to see fairies, and there they are, having a perfectly lovely time in our palace of bricks. What a good thing we left the bricks here!'

Suddenly one of the pixies gave a scream and pointed to the two children who were bending down to peep in at the windows.

'Look!' she cried. 'Oh, look! Quick, run away, everybody!'

'No, please don't,' said Donald, politely. 'We're very glad indeed to see you using our palace. We remembered that we had left it outside in the rain so we came to put away the bricks – and we saw you. But please go on with your party!'

'Oh, do you mind?' asked the Princess Peronel, coming to the door and looking up at the children. 'It was such a wet night, we couldn't dance out-of-doors – so when we found this perfectly lovely palace we thought we'd use it. But do you think the rain will hurt it?'

'Never mind if it does,' said Donald. 'We wouldn't dream of putting the bricks away now.'

'It's very kind of you,' said the Princess. 'I'll tell you what we'll do for you. We will send the sun brownies to dry every single bit of the palace at dawn, and when you come out in the morning, you will see it is all quite dry, and no harm will come to the bricks.'

'Thank you,' said Mary gratefully. 'That is very nice of you. Good night – we won't stay any longer because we're getting wet!'

Back to the bedroom they went, most excited, and they talked hard about their adventure until they fell asleep. In the morning they raced out to the garden.

There was their palace, as dry as could be, shining in the sunshine! Not a single brick was wet!

They told their mother all about it, but she laughed and said they must have dreamt it.

'We *couldn't* have dreamt it, could we, Mary?' said Donald as they slowly took down the palace to put away the bricks. 'Oh, I say – look here!'

He picked up a little golden dish of the tiniest cakes you could imagine!

'The pixies left these behind!' he said. 'Let's

go and show Mummy! She'll believe us then.'

And she did! The two children are going to eat the cakes for their tea. I do wonder what will happen when they do, don't you?

Jeanie's Monkey

There was once upon a time a little girl called Jeanie, who had a great many pets. She had a dog called Pip, a cat called Whiskers, two guinea-pigs called Bubble and Squeak, and a small toad that lived under the garden step. So you see she had a great many creatures to look after.

What she longed to have was a little monkey! She thought it would be lovely to have a small brown monkey that would play with her and Pip. But her Mummy said no, she had quite enough pets.

One day Jeanie was lying on the grass playing with Whiskers, when she suddenly saw a four-leaved clover. Now these are very lucky, as you know, and Jeanie was delighted. She knew that if she tied it on a thread and wore it round her neck all day, she could wish a wish and it might come true. For four-leaved clovers are magic and belong to the fairies.

Jeanie picked the clover-leaf and looked at it carefully to make sure there was no mistake. It was quite right – it had four leaves as plain as anything. Jeanie ran indoors and showed her mother. Then she took a piece of black cotton and tied the clover-leaf carefully to it. She wore it round her neck the whole day long – and what do you suppose she wished?

'I wish I could have a little brown monkey,' she said to herself all day long, wishing as hard as she could.

But no monkey came. Jeanie was most disappointed and she went to bed thinking that four-leaved clovers couldn't be magic after all. And then, just as she was falling asleep, she heard a funny little sound in the day nursery, next to her bedroom.

She sat up and listened. It was a little chattering noise. Jeanie couldn't think *what* it could be!

'I'll go and see!' she thought, and she popped out of bed and ran into the day nursery. She *was* astonished at what she found there.

The chattering noise came from the corner where the doll's cot stood – and there, cuddling into the cot, was a small brown monkey!

'My dream's come true!' cried Jeanie in delight, and she ran across to the monkey. He put out a tiny paw, just like a hand and stroked her. Then he cuddled down into the doll's cot again. He was shivering with cold.

'You poor little thing!' cried Jeanie. 'You are so cold! I'll get you a woolly coat that belongs to my big teddy bear. That will keep you warm.'

So she got the warm red coat and put it on the monkey. He was so pleased. Then Jeanie tucked him up in the cot and told him to go to sleep till morning.

He cuddled down and closed his eyes. Jeanie ran back to bed, very happy. Her dream had come true. Four-leaved clovers were magic, after all!

Next morning she went to look for the monkey and found him still fast asleep in the cot. She wondered what he would like for his breakfast, and she remembered that monkeys like bananas. So she ran to the cupboard where Mummy kept the fruit and took a banana. She peeled it and put it on a plate. The little monkey soon woke up when she patted him, and sat up in the cot. He was delighted to see the banana, and took it off the plate.

'Chitter-chitter, chatter, chitter!' he said, in his little chattery voice. He held the banana in his paw and bit big pieces off it, looking at Jeanie with his bright eyes as he ate. She thought he was the dearest little monkey in the world.

'You look rather dirty,' she said. 'I think I will give you a good wash. And see – your hind paw is hurt. I will wrap it up in a bandage for you.'

Just then Mummy called her to breakfast and she ran off. She chattered all about the monkey whilst she had her breakfast, but her mother thought she was talking about a toy monkey she had, and took no notice. Jeanie ran back after her breakfast and got her doll's bath ready. She filled it full of nice hot water and made it soapy. Then she got an old nail brush and called the monkey. He came at once.

He didn't like the bath very much, but he *did* look nice and clean afterwards. Jeanie scrubbed him with the nail brush and then rubbed him dry with an old towel. She put on the little coat again, and tied a scarf round his neck. Then she put him down in the sun, and he fell asleep again. He really was a dear little monkey, and he seemed quite a baby one.

Before he fell asleep Jeanie bound up his paw, which was cut, and he was very pleased with the bandage. He kept looking at it until he fell asleep. Jeanie put him in her doll's pram and thought she would take him for a walk. She took him into the garden and walked round and round with him. When he woke up he was quite ready for a game.

You should have seen that monkey playing! He pulled Pip's tail, he climbed all the trees, he chattered to Whiskers, who was half afraid of him, and he kept jumping on to Jeanie's shoulder and pulling off her hair-slide.

He really was the most mischievous little creature!

When Mummy came out into the garden she stared in the greatest astonishment at the monkey. She really could hardly believe her eyes.

'Jeanie!' she cried. 'Where did that monkey come from?'

'It's the one I told you about at breakfast-time this morning,' said Jeanie.

'But I thought you were talking about your *toy* monkey then!' said her mother. 'Where did this little creature come from?'

'I wished for him and he came,' said Jeanie. 'I found a four-leaved clover, you see, Mummy.'

Well, her mother was as puzzled as could be. She kept saying that the monkey must have escaped from somewhere, and Jeanie really couldn't keep him. And Jeanie kept saying that it was *her* monkey because she had wished him and he had come.

When Cook saw the monkey she said she knew where he came from.

'I'm sure it's the monkey I saw on the barrel-organ belonging to the Italian who used to play down our street at home,' she said. 'I've often seen the cruel man beating him, poor little monkey. He's only a young monkey, and a gentle creature, too.'

'Well, we must find out if it *does* belong to the organ-grinder,' said Mummy. But Jeanie began to cry when she heard that.

'It's *my* monkey!' she said. 'It doesn't belong to the organ-grinder. I wished him and he came.'

But, you know, he *did* belong to the

83

organ-grinder, because when Daddy began to try to find out about him, a policeman told him that the Italian had lost his monkey.

'Oh, he can't go back to that horrid man!' wept Jeanie, hugging the little monkey to her. 'I won't have him beaten, poor little thing. He's so gentle and sweet.'

'I'll go and see the organ-grinder and find out what he says,' said Daddy. So off he went. He soon found out where the man lived, and knocked at the door.

The Italian lived in two dirty little rooms, and when he heard that his monkey had been found he wanted it back at once.

'It is a silly, weak animal,' he said. 'I do not like it. It has to be beaten every day because it will not learn to take round my hat for pennies.'

'Well, if you like I will buy it from you for my little girl,' said Daddy. 'She likes it, and it seems happy with her. If you take it back it will probably catch a cold and die.'

'You give me four shillings and you can have the silly little animal,' said the organ-grinder at once. Daddy paid him four shillings and went home. He called Jeanie as soon as he got back. She came running to him, hugging the little monkey, her eyes full of tears because she thought her Daddy was going to take it back to the organ-grinder.

'Cheer up, Jeanie,' said Daddy. 'The organ-grinder doesn't want the monkey. You can keep it! Look after it well, for it is not very strong and has been badly treated.'

Well, you should have seen Jeanie's face! It was as bright as the sun! She hugged her Daddy, she hugged her Mummy, she hugged the monkey!

'I knew he was mine!' she cried. 'I wished him and he came. I knew he was mine! The fairies knew he was unhappy, so when they heard my monkey-wish, they took him away from the unkind organ-grinder and brought him to my nursery. They did, Mummy, truly, because you know I found a four-leaved clover, and that's magic! Oh, I am so glad to have him for a pet!'

The monkey still lives with Jeanie and Pip and Whiskers. You'll see him if ever you go to tea. He is a real little mischief, and he will take your handkerchief out of your pocket whenever you are not looking. So be careful when you play with him!

Thimble's Whirlwind

Once upon a time, in the village of Go-and-See there lived a big, fat gnome called Brin-Brin. He was very proud and haughty, always rude to everyone, and thought such a lot of himself, that nobody dared to speak to him unless he spoke first.

Next door to Brin-Brin lived a tiny pixie, called Thimble. He didn't like being next door to Brin-Brin at all. For one thing the big gnome threw all his rubbish over the wall into Thimble's garden, and he was always having to clear up tins, bottles and potato parings. It was a great nuisance. But he didn't like to complain.

Another thing was that Brin-Brin often used to sing very loudly, and as he had a dreadful voice, it was very painful for Thimble to have to sit and listen to it.

He would shut his windows to keep the sound out, but as soon as Brin-Brin saw him doing that he would sing twice as loudly as before, so it was really worse.

Thimble was a good-natured little pixie, and he would have liked to be friendly to Brin-Brin, but it was quite impossible. He really was a horrid person, and he ate so much that poor Thimble's garden was always full of rubbishy tins and pots thrown over the wall by the greedy gnome.

Thimble felt one day that he really could *not* put up with Brin-Brin any longer. So he sat on his three-legged stool and tried to think of a

plan to get rid of him. It was very difficult —
but at last he thought of one. He waited until a
windy day came, and he watched for Brin-Brin
to set out on his usual walk through Red-Leaf
Woods.

Then he followed after him. Brin-Brin
walked on, crunching the dead leaves under
his feet, for it was autumn. Behind him came
Thimble. Brin-Brin sat down at the foot of a
tree and unwrapped a parcel of sticky buns
that he was going to eat.

Thimble waited a little while behind another
tree a little way off. Then he suddenly began to
cry out loudly: 'Help! Help! There's a great, big
whirlwind coming! Help! Help!'

Then Thimble started to run towards Brin-
Brin as if there was a wind behind him, blowing
him along. He shot by Brin-Brin, clutched
hold of a tree and cried: 'Help! Help! There's a
great big whirlwind coming! It nearly blew me
away then.'

Brin-Brin was so astonished that he dropped two of his buns to the ground. He stared at Thimble in a great fright, his big mouth wide open. Once a whirlwind had come to the village of Go-and-See and had blown off all the chimney-pots, and ever since then Brin-Brin had been very much afraid of a storm.

'Oh, is that you, Brin-Brin!' shouted Thimble, pretending that he saw the gnome for the first time. 'You hold on to a tree like I'm doing! Quick! The whirlwind might come at any minute and blow you away to the moon!'

Brin-Brin jumped up, shaking like a jelly, and held on to the tree behind him. At the same moment a little wind blew the dry leaves about, and Brin-Brin shouted in terror, for he really thought it was the beginning of the whirlwind. He clung to his tree tightly.

'Oh, Brin-Brin,' said Thimble, 'what a pity you are so fat! The whirlwind will easily be able to take you away, and will bowl you along like a piece of paper. If you were small like me, you would be all right, for the wind would hardly notice you.'

'D-d-d-d-do you th-th-think s-s-so?' said poor Brin-Brin, his teeth chattering so much that he could hardly talk. 'Oh, whatever shall I do? I shall never be able to hold on long enough to this tree.'

'I've a piece of rope here,' said Thimble, at once. 'Shall I tie you tightly to the tree? Then the whirlwind won't be able to blow you away, however much it tries.'

'Oh, do, do!' begged Brin-Brin. 'Quick, before it starts!'

Thimble ran over to Brin-Brin. The wind blew a little again, and Brin-Brin gave a cry of fright.

'Quick! Tie me up! The whirlwind is beginning!'

Thimble grinned to himself, and very quickly he tied Brin-Brin to the tree. How tightly he

91

tied him! You should have seen the knots. My goodness, they would have held an elephant!

'There!' said Thimble, stepping back to look at Brin-Brin. 'You're nicely tied up!'

'Come back and hold to a tree!' cried Brin-Brin. 'You'll be blown away.'

'Oh, *I'm* not afraid of a silly old whirlwind,' said Thimble, and to Brin-Brin's great astonishment he walked away, leaving the gnome alone.

But not for long! Oh no, there was soon quite a crowd round Brin-Brin, for Thimble had fetched all the village along to see him.

'However did you manage to conquer Brin-Brin and tie him up like that?' cried all the little folk. 'Did you fight him, Thimble? Oh, how clever you are! How strong! How wonderful! Tell us all about it.'

'Oh, there's nothing to tell,' said Thimble airily. 'Nothing at all. I thought it was time that Brin-Brin was punished, so I tied him up for everyone to see.'

Well, you should have seen Brin-Brin's face when he heard all this! He simply didn't know what to say!

'I'm tied up be-because there's a whirlwind c-c-coming,' he said at last. 'That's all.'

'Ha, ha, ho, ho!' laughed all the little folk. 'What a joke! A whirlwind indeed! Whoever heard of such an excuse! Ho ho!'

'Ho, ho, ho!' laughed Thimble, loudest of all.

Brin-Brin tried to get loose but Thimble had tied him up far too tightly. He was so angry that his face was as red as a ripe tomato. How dared Thimble play this trick on him! Just wait! He would punish him when he got free!

But when would he get free? Nobody offered to untie him. When night came and they were tired of laughing at him they all went home, except Thimble.

'They'll come back to laugh at you again tomorrow,' said Thimble. 'What a pity you have always been so proud and haughty, rude and selfish, Brin-Brin! If you hadn't been, you might have found someone kind enough to set you free.'

'Please set me free yourself,' said Brin-Brin, in a humble voice.

'What! Set you free to rush at me and hit

me!' said Thimble. 'No, no, Brin-Brin – I'm not as foolish as that.'

Then Brin-Brin saw that things were really very serious. He might stay a prisoner for weeks. He must humble himself to the clever little pixie.

'Please, Thimble,' he begged. 'Set me free. I will promise not to hurt you. I have been a stupid, proud gnome, but I will never be again.'

'Will you pack your bags and go away if I set you free?' asked Thimble.

'Yes,' said Brin-Brin, at once, thinking that he certainly could never face seeing all the people of Go-and-See Village again. No – they would always laugh at him now. He must certainly go right away and never come back.

That was just what Thimble wanted! He at once ran to Brin-Brin and untied him. The gnome stretched his arms and legs and then set off in silence to his house. He packed up his bags and left his house that night, walking steadily towards the silver moon.

Thimble watched him go in delight. He had got rid of his unpleasant neighbour. Never again would he find his garden full of rubbish! Never again would he hear a voice singing loudly next door. Ho, ho, ho!

'Where has Brin-Brin gone?' asked the little folk next day.

'Oh, I untied him, told him to pack his bags and go,' said Thimble. 'So he's gone.'

'Dear, dear, what a wonder you are!' said the little folk, in delight. 'Let's hope he'll never come back!'

He never did – and I don't expect he ever will, do you?

A Shock for Freddie

There was once a little girl called Linda. She lived in a small cottage with her mother and father, and she was very fond of gardening. So her mother bought her a watering-can, a trowel, a fork, a broom and rake for her very own.

'You can keep them in the apple-shed,' said her mother, 'then they won't get mixed up with Daddy's things. There is plenty of room behind the apple-racks.'

So Linda kept her tools there. She was a

very good worker, and she always kept her tools clean and tidy. She never put any of them away dirty, and she used to rub the trowel and fork till they shone before she put them away.

They often used to talk about Linda, in the middle of the night, when they were all alone in the sweet-smelling apple-shed.

'She's a very nice child to belong to,' said the broom in its funny sweeping voice.

'She looks after us so well,' said the trowel, in its scrapy voice.

'Not like the boy next door,' said the watering-can. 'He simply throws his tools into the shed all dirty, and never cleans them at all. They are rusty, and three of them are broken.'

'His watering-can has a hole in the bottom,' said the rake.

'How dreadful!' said Linda's can, shivering on its shelf.

'His fork is broken,' said the broom.

'Dear, dear, what a horrid boy!' said Linda's

fork. 'I *am* glad we don't belong to him! I hope he never comes here.'

Well, one day the boy next door *did* come to Linda's garden. His name was Freddie, and he was a fat, lazy boy, clumsy and careless. On the other side of the fence there was a little shed just like Linda's apple-shed, and one day when Freddie was peeping through the cracks in the side of it, he found that he could see right into the apple-shed next door.

And his greedy little eyes saw the red apples stored so carefully in the apple-racks there! Goodness me, how his mouth watered when he saw them!

'I shall wait until Linda and everyone next door are out,' said Freddie to himself, 'and then I shall climb over the fence, squeeze in at the shed window and eat a few apples. Nobody will know, and I shall have a fine feast.'

Well, that is exactly what he *did* do! The very next day he watched Linda and her father and mother go out to tea, and as soon as they were gone he climbed quickly over the fence and ran to the apple-shed. The door was locked, as he had thought it would be, but it didn't take him a minute to open the little window and squeeze himself through it.

Then what a fine time he had! He ate four of the biggest, reddest apples, and then climbed out of the window again, with two apples safely in his pocket.

The tools on the shelf behind the apples looked at one another in anger. How dare that horrid boy come into their shed and steal their apples?

'Linda will be blamed for taking them,' said the fork in a rage. 'She is the only person who comes here besides her mother and father.'

The fork was right. Linda *was* blamed for taking the apples, and she was very sad about it.

'But, Mummy, I didn't *touch* the apples,'

she said. 'Truly I didn't. I would never take anything you told me not to, really I wouldn't.'

'Well, who *did* take them then?' said her mother. 'The door is always locked.'

The next week Freddie took some more apples, and Linda was scolded again. She cried bitterly and was very unhappy. The tools longed to tell her who the thief was, but they couldn't talk as she did. It was dreadful.

Then the broom had a wonderful idea.

'Let's punish Freddie and give him such a fright that he will never come to our shed again!' it said. 'I will sweep him off his feet, and you, watering-can, can water him from head to foot.'

'And I will rake him up and down,' said the rake.

'And we will dig under his toes and make holes for him to fall into,' said the fork and trowel in excitement. 'He deserves to be punished. Watering-can, it's pouring with rain now, so if you stick yourself out of the window, you will get full of raindrops – then you will be ready for Freddie!'

'Ready for Freddie!' sang all the tools, in glee.

Now it so happened that night that Freddie was sent to bed without any supper because he had been naughty. So he was very hungry indeed. He hadn't been in bed very long before he made up his mind to steal downstairs, climb over the garden-wall, and go to the apple-shed next door. Then he would eat plenty of those lovely red apples there!

So off he went, and it wasn't long before he was in the shed. The tools felt most excited. Now they could do all they had planned to do!

Freddie felt about for the apple-racks. Then he quickly took four apples and stuffed them into a bag he had brought with him – and just as he did that, the watering-can carefully tipped itself up and began to water him!

'Ooh!' shouted Freddie in a fright, as the cold

102

water soaked him from head to foot. 'What is it? Ooh! Stop!'

But the watering-can didn't stop until it had emptied all its water on to the frightened little thief. Then it was the rake's turn! It jumped up to Freddie and began to rake him up and down, tearing big holes in his sleeping-suit. Freddie tried to run away from it, but the fork and trowel hopped about in front of him, digging little holes under his toes.

'There are rats round my feet!' cried Freddie. 'Help! Help!'

Then the broom thought it would join in, and it began to sweep Freddie up as if he were dead leaves. Swish! Swish! Freddie called for help even more loudly, and this time Linda's father and mother heard him and came rushing out to the apple-shed to see what was the matter.

When they saw Freddie with the bag of apples in his hand they knew at once who had been the apple-thief. They took Freddie into their cottage and looked at him. He was wet, dirty and torn, and he cried with fright.

'What *have* you been doing in that shed?' asked Linda, peeping down the stairs in surprise.

'S-s-something w-w-watered me!' sobbed Freddie.

'My watering-can!' cried Linda.

'And then something raked me up and down!' wept Freddie.

'My garden rake!' said Linda.

'And rats kept digging holes under my feet, and then something swept me up!' sobbed the frightened boy.

'My fork and trowel and my broom!' cried

Linda. 'They must have seen you stealing our apples and felt cross with you. Well, it serves you right.'

'Don't punish me for taking your apples,' begged Freddie, turning to Linda's father and mother.

'You have been well punished already,' said Linda's mother. 'Go back now to your own house. I am afraid that when your mother sees your torn sleeping-suit she will be very cross with you.'

So she was! Poor Freddie was well spanked and as he lay in bed again that night, he said to himself: 'Well, that's the last time I ever take anything that doesn't belong to me! I wonder what it was that treated me like that in the apple-shed. It couldn't *really* have been Linda's tools.'

But it was! Linda knew it and she thanked them very much next time she used them – and how she cleans and polishes them! They really are a wonderful sight to see.

The Three Naughty Children

One day Queen Peronel's cook heard a knocking at her kitchen door. She opened it and saw a ragged pedlar there, his tray of goods in front of him.

'Can I sell you something?' said the pedlar. 'Red ribbons, silver thimbles, honey-chocolate, high-heeled shoes – I have them all here.'

'Nothing today, thank you,' said the cook. But the pedlar would not go.

'I am tired with walking many miles,' he said. 'Let me come in and rest a little. See, I will wipe my feet well on the mat so that I shall not dirty your clean kitchen floor.'

So the cook let him come in and sit down on her oldest chair for a little while. But when he had gone she missed three things, and flew to tell Queen Peronel.

'Oh, Your Highness!' she cried, bursting into the drawing-room where the Queen sat knitting a jersey. 'Oh, Your Highness, a pedlar has stolen your blue milk-jug, your little silver spoon and your wooden porridge plate! Oh, whatever shall I do!'

Now these three things were all full of magic and the Queen treasured them very much. The blue milk-jug had the power of pouring out perfectly fresh milk twice a day, which was very useful for the Queen's nurse, for she had two little princesses and a prince to look after in the royal nursery. The silver spoon would make anyone hungry if he put it into his mouth, and this, too, was *very* useful if any of the royal children wouldn't eat a meal.

The wooden porridge plate could play a tune all the time that porridge was eaten from it, so the children loved it very much. Queen Peronel was dreadfully upset when she heard that all these things had been stolen.

'What was the pedlar like?' she asked. 'I will have him captured and put into prison.'

But alas, when the cook told her about the pedlar's looks, the Queen knew that he was no pedlar but a wizard who had dressed himself up to steal her treasures. She called the King and he really didn't know what to do.

'That wizard is too powerful for us to send to prison,' he said, shaking his head. 'He won't give us back those three things if we ask him nicely, for he will say he didn't steal them. I really do *not* know what to do.'

Now when the two little princesses and the prince heard how the wizard had stolen their milk-jug, porridge plate and spoon, they were very angry.

'Send a hundred soldiers to him, Father, and capture him!' cried Roland, the little prince, standing straight and tall in front of the King.

'Don't be silly, my dear child,' said the King. 'He would turn them all into wolves and send them howling back here. You wouldn't like that, would you?'

'Well, Father, send someone to steal all the things from *him*,' said Rosalind, the eldest child, throwing back her golden curls.

'You don't know what you are talking about,' said the King crossly. 'Go back to the nursery, all of you, and play at trains.'

They went back to the nursery, but they didn't play at trains. They sat in a corner and talked. Rosalind and Roland were very fierce about the stealing of their magic things. Then Roland suddenly thought of an idea.

'I say, Rosalind, what about dressing up as a

wizard myself and going to call on the wizard who took away our things? Perhaps I could make him give them back. *I'm* not afraid of any old wizard!'

'I shall come, too,' said Rosalind, who liked to be in everything.

'And so shall I,' said Goldilocks, the youngest of them all.

'You're too little,' said Roland.

'I'm *not!*' said Goldilocks. 'I shall cry if you don't let me come.'

'All right, all right, you can come,' said Roland, 'but if you get turned into a worm or something, don't blame *me!*'

Then they made their plans, and very peculiar plans they were, too. They were all to slip out of bed that night and go downstairs, dressed, when nobody was about. Roland was to get his father's grandest cloak and feathered hat, and the two girls were to take with them a pair of bellows each, a box of fireworks from the firework cupboard, and two watering-cans full of water. How strange!

They were most excited. They could hardly wait until the clock struck eleven and everyone else was in bed. Then they dressed and went downstairs. Soon Roland was wrapped in his father's wonderful gold and silver cloak, with big diamonds at the neck and round the hem. On his curly head he put his father's magnificent feathered hat, stuffed with a piece of paper inside to make it fit. Then, with their burden of bellows, fireworks and watering-cans, they set off to the wizard's little house on the hillside not far off.

It was all in darkness save for one light in the nearest window.

'He's still up,' said Roland. 'Good! Now, you two girls, you know what to do, don't you? As soon as you hear me shouting up the chimney, do your part. And if you make a mistake, Goldilocks, I'll pull your hair tomorrow, so there!'

'Help me to get the ladder out of the garden shed,' said Rosalind as they came near to the cottage. Roland and the two girls silently carried the ladder to the cottage and placed it softly against the roof. Then up went the two princesses, as quietly as cats. In half a minute they were sitting beside the chimney, their bellows, fireworks and watering-cans beside them.

It was time for Roland to do his part. He wrapped the big cloak around his shoulder and strode up to the door. He hammered on it with a stone he had picked up and made a tremendous noise. The wizard inside nearly jumped out of his skin.

'Now who can this be?' he wondered, getting up. 'Some great witch or enchanter, hammering like that on my door!'

He opened the door and Roland strode in, not a bit nervous.

'Good evening, wizard,' he said. 'I am Rilloby-

Rimmony-Ru, the Enchanter from the moon. I have heard that you can do wondrous things. Show me some.'

The wizard looked at Roland's grand cloak and hat and thought he must indeed be a rich and great enchanter. He bowed low.

'I can command gold to come from the air, silver to come from the streams, and music from the stars,' he said.

'Pooh!' said Roland rudely. 'Anyone can do that! Can you call the wind and make it do your bidding?'

'Great sir, no one can do that,' answered the wizard, mockingly.

'Ho, you mock at me, do you?' said Roland. He went to the chimney and shouted up it. 'Wind, come down to me and show this poor wizard how you obey my commands!'

At once Rosalind and Goldilocks began to work the bellows down the chimney, blowing great puffs of air down as they opened and shut the bellows. The smoke from the fire was blown all over the room and the wizard began to cough. He looked frightened.

'Enough, enough!' he cried. 'You will smoke me out. Command the wind to stop blowing down my chimney.'

'Stop blowing, wind!' commanded Roland,

shouting up the chimney. At once the two girls on the roof stopped working the bellows, and the smoke went up the chimney in the ordinary way.

'Wonderful, wonderful!' said the wizard, staring at Roland in amazement. 'I have never seen anyone make the wind his servant before.'

'That's nothing,' said Roland, grandly. 'I can command the rain, too.'

'Bid it come, then,' said the wizard, trembling. Roland shouted up the chimney. 'Rain, come at my bidding!' At once Rosalind and Goldilocks poured water down the chimney from their watering-cans and it hissed on the fire and spat out on the hearth. The wizard leapt back in alarm.

'Stop the rain!' he cried. 'It will put out my fire if it rushes down my chimney like that.'

Roland, who didn't at all want the fire to be put out, hastily shouted to the rain to stop, and the two little girls put their watering-cans down, giggling to hear the astonished cries of the wizard.

'Surely you can do no greater thing than these!' said the wizard to Roland.

'Well, I can command the thunder and lightning, too,' said Roland. 'Wait. I will call down some for you to see.'

Before the frightened wizard could stop him Roland shouted up the chimney again. 'Thunder and lightning, come down here!'

Rosalind dropped a handful of fireworks down at once. They fell into the flames and exploded with an enormous bang, flashing brightly. The wizard yelled in alarm and ran into a corner. Rosalind dropped down some more fireworks, and two squibs hopped right out of the fire to the corner where the wizard was hiding.

'Oh, oh, the thunderstorm is coming after me!' he shouted. 'Take it away, great Enchanter, take it away!'

Roland badly wanted to laugh, but he dared

not even smile. Another batch of fireworks fell down the chimney, and the wizard rushed away again and fell over a stool.

'Stop, thunder and lightning!' called Roland up the chimney. At once the girls stopped throwing down fireworks and there was peace and quiet in the room, save for the wizard's moans of fright.

'Am I not a powerful enchanter?' asked Roland, grandly. 'Would you not like to know my secrets?'

'Oh, Master, would you tell me them?' cried the wizard, delighted.

'I will write them down on a piece of paper for you,' said Roland, 'but you must not look at it until tomorrow morning. And now, what will you give me in return?'

'Sacks of gold, cart-loads of silver,' cried the grateful wizard.

'Pooh!' said Roland, scornfully. 'What's the use of those to me? I am richer than everyone in the world put together.'

'Then look round my humble dwelling and choose what takes your fancy,' said the wizard at once. 'See, I have strange things here – what would you like?'

Roland glanced round quickly and saw the blue milk-jug, the silver spoon and the porridge plate on a shelf.

'Hm!' he said. 'I don't see much that I like. Wait! Here is a pretty jug. I will take that in return for the secret of the wind. And here is a dainty silver spoon. That shall be my reward for the secret of the rain. Then what shall I take for the secret of the thunder and lightning? Ah, here is a porridge plate I shall love to use. Wizard, I will take all these. Now see – here is an envelope. Inside you will find written the secret of the wind, the rain and the thunderstorm you have seen here tonight. Do not open it until tomorrow morning.'

He took the jug, the spoon and the porridge

dish, and strode out of the door, the wizard bowing respectfully in front of him. Rosalind and Goldilocks had already climbed down the ladder and were waiting for him. They ran as fast as they could with all their watering-cans, bellows and other things, laughing till they cried when they thought of the clever tricks they had played.

And when the King and Queen heard of their prank they didn't know whether to scold or praise.

'You naughty, brave, rascally, daring scamps!' cried the Queen. 'Why, you might have been turned into frogs!'

As for the wizard, when he opened the envelope the next morning and saw what was written there, he was very puzzled indeed. For this is what Roland had written: 'The secret of the wind is Bellows. The secret of the rain is Watering-cans. The secret of the thunderstorm is Fireworks. Ha! ha!'

And now the poor wizard is wandering all over the world trying to find someone wise and clever enough to tell him the meaning of the Bellows, the Watering-cans and the Fireworks, But nobody likes to!

The Two Good Fairies

David and Ruth lived in Primrose Cottage, and next door to them was Daffodil Cottage. An old man lived there, very fond of his garden, which was just a little piece like theirs.

One day the old man fell ill and had to go away to be nursed. David and Ruth peeped over the fence at his garden, which was full of daffodils and primroses.

'Old Mr Reed will be sorry to leave his lovely daffodils before they are over,' said Ruth. 'I wonder if his servant will look

121

after his garden for him.'

'Mr Reed was a cross old man,' said David. 'He used to frown if we shouted or made a noise.'

'And he hated to let us get a ball if it went over the fence,' said Ruth.

'He was never well,' said their mother. 'That is why he was cross. I expect if he had been well and strong like you he would have been jolly and good-tempered.'

The cottage next door was shut up and the hard-working little servant went back to her mother. There was no one to look after the garden, and as soon as the daffodils and primroses were over, the garden beds became full of weeds. The little lawn grew long and untidy, and thistles grew at the end of the garden.

'Isn't it a pity?' said Ruth, looking over the fence at the untidy garden. 'It used to be so nice in the summertime, full of flowers. Now it is like a field!'

'I wonder when old Mr Reed will come back,' said David.

'Mother says he is coming back in June,' said Ruth. 'Our garden will look lovely then, but his will be dreadful.'

'Let's go and buy our seeds tomorrow,' said David. 'We ought to be planting them now, you know, else our gardens will be late with their summer flowers.'

They emptied out their money-box and counted their money. They had plenty to buy seeds.

'I wish we had enough to buy a nice wheelbarrow, a new watering-can and a spade,' said David longingly. 'All our garden things are getting old. Shall we ask Mother if she'll buy us some new ones?'

But Mother said no. 'I can't afford it,' she said. 'I am saving up to buy a new hoover, because mine is falling to bits. I'll see about your garden tools after I've bought a new hoover.'

'Oh dear,' said Ruth, 'that won't be for ages!'

The two children went off to the seedsman to buy their garden seeds. They bought candytuft, poppies, nasturtiums, Virginia stock, love-in-a-mist and cornflowers – all the things that most children love to grow in their gardens. Then back they went to plant them.

They were very good little gardeners. They knew just how to get the beds ready, and how to shake the seed gently out of the packets so that not too much went into one place. They watered their seeds carefully and kept the weeds from the beds. Mother was quite proud of the way they kept their little gardens.

As they were planting their seeds Ruth had a good idea. She sat back on the grass and told it to David.

'I say, David, we've plenty of seeds this year, haven't we?' she said. 'Well, let's go and plant some next door in the little round bed just in front of the window where the old man sits

every day. Even if his garden is in a dreadful
state he will be able to see one nice flowery bed!
It would be such a nice surprise for him!'

David thought it was a good idea. So when
they had finished planting their seeds in their
own little gardens the two children ran into
the garden next door. Then they began to work
very hard indeed.

The round bed was covered with weeds!
So before any seeds were planted all the
dandelions, buttercups and other weeds had to

be dug up and taken away. Then the bed was dug well over by David, and Ruth made the earth nice and fine.

Then they planted the seeds. In the middle they put cornflowers because they were nice and tall. Round them they put candytuft, with poppies here and there. In front they put love-in-a-mist with nasturtiums in between, and to edge the bed they planted seeds of the gay little Virginia stock. They were so pleased when they had finished, for the bed looked very neat and tidy.

There! That's finished,' said David. 'Now we've only got to come in and weed and water, and the bed will look lovely in the summertime! How surprised old Mr Reed will be!'

You should have seen how those seeds grew. It was wonderful. The children's gardens looked pretty enough, but the round bed next door was marvellous.

The cornflowers were the deepest of blues,

and the candytuft was strong and sturdy. The Virginia stock was full of buds.

'Old Mr Reed is coming back tomorrow,' said Ruth in excitement. 'Won't he be surprised!'

He did come back – and he *was* surprised! The children peeped over the fence and saw him looking out of his window in the very greatest astonishment. He saw them and waved to them.

'Hallo, Ruth and David,' he said. 'Just look at that round bed! Isn't it a picture? I was so sad when I came back thinking that I wouldn't have any flowers in my garden this summer – and the first thing I saw was this lovely bed full of colour. Do *you* know who planted the seeds?'

David and Ruth didn't like to say that they had done it.

'Perhaps it was the fairies,' said Mr Reed. 'I shouldn't be a bit surprised, would you? Well, I shall have to reward them for such a kind deed. I wonder whether one of you would come over tonight after the sun has gone down and water the bed for me? I don't expect the fairies will come now I'm back, do you?'

That evening the children took their old leaky watering-can next door and went to water the round bed. Mr Reed watched them from the window. Ruth and David saw something by the bed – and what do you think it was?

There was a fine new wheelbarrow, and inside it were two strong spades and a perfectly splendid new red watering-can. There was a note inside the barrow too, that said: 'A present for the kind fairies who gave me such a nice surprise.'

The children didn't know *what* to do. Did Mr Reed really think it was the fairies that had worked so hard? Oh, what lovely garden tools these were – just what they needed so badly. They stood and looked at them.

'How do you like your new tools?' shouted Mr Reed from his window.

'Oh, are they for *us?*' cried the children in delight. 'It says in the note that they are for the good fairies.'

'Well, didn't you act like good fairies?' said the old man, smiling. 'You gave me a wonderful surprise, and now I'm giving you one. You did a very kind deed to a cross, bad-tempered old man. But I'm better now, and so is my temper, especially since I've had such a lovely surprise. So I hope you will often come to tea with me and play with the new puppy I have bought. Now water my garden and then take your things home to show your mother.'

'Oh, thank you *so* much,' said the children, so excited that they could hardly hold the watering-can properly. Whatever would Mother say when she heard what had happened?

Mother was delighted.

'You deserve your surprise,' she said. 'You were kind to someone you didn't very much like, and now you have made a friend and had a lovely present.'

You should see David and Ruth gardening now with all their new tools. They are as happy as can be – and all because Ruth had a good idea and was kind to a cross old man.

The Newspaper Dog

Once upon a time there was a little dog called Tips. He belonged to Mrs Brown who lived in Primrose Cottage at the end of Cherry Village.

He was a useful little dog. He guarded the house each night for Mrs Brown. He kept her company when she was alone. He barked at any tramp who came up the front path – and once each week he fetched a newspaper for her from old Mr Jonathan who lived all by himself in a little house on the hillside.

Mr Jonathan bought the newspaper himself,

and read it. Then he lent it to Mrs Jones, and after that she passed it on to someone else. She couldn't often find time to go to fetch the paper herself, so Tips fetched it for her.

He started off each Thursday evening, ran all the way down the village street, went over the bridge that crossed the stream and up the hillside to Mr Jonathan's cottage. He jumped up at the door and pushed it open. Then in he would trot and look for Mr Jonathan.

The old man always had the paper ready for him, neatly folded up with a piece of string round it. He put the packet into Tips's mouth and off the little dog would go, running all the way home again, not stopping for anything until he reached Primrose Cottage and could drop the paper at Mrs Jones's feet.

One day Mr Jonathan thought he would do some spring-cleaning. So he called on Mrs Jones and asked her to lend him her ladder.

'Dear me, what do you want to go climbing

about on ladders for?' asked Mrs Jones in surprise. 'You'll fall off, Mr Jonathan, and hurt yourself.'

'Indeed I shan't!' said the old man. 'I'm going to paint my ceiling white, Mrs Jones. It is very dirty. So lend me your step-ladder, there's a good soul.'

'It's in the shed,' said Mrs Jones. 'You can have it if you want it. But do pray be careful, Mr Jonathan, for it's not a very steady pair of steps.'

Mr Jonathan found the ladder and took it home. He mixed some whitening and started to do his ceiling. It looked lovely! All day he worked at it, and then went to bed.

He began again next day, whistling to himself, sloshing about on the ceiling with the whitewash, quite enjoying himself. And then a dreadful thing happened.

The postman dropped some letters in the letterbox and gave such a loud rat-a-tat that the shock made old Mr Jonathan fall off his ladder. Down he went – and when he tried to get up he found that he couldn't.

'Oh dear, oh dear, I must have sprained my ankle, or broken my leg, or something,' the old man groaned. 'Whatever shall I do? Nobody else will come today, and I can't send anyone for the doctor. I have no neighbours to call to. I am all alone!'

He lay there on the floor, groaning. He really didn't know what he was going to do. Perhaps he would have to stay there all night long. If only somebody would come! But there was nobody to come at all.

And then, just as he was thinking that, Mr Jonathan heard the sound of pitter-pattering feet, and someone came running up the front path. Then a little body hurled itself against the door which opened at once. It was Tips, the little newspaper dog, come to get his mistress's paper, for it was Thursday evening!

He saw Mr Jonathan lying on the floor, and he was puzzled. He ran up to him and licked his hand. Then he sat down with his head on one side and said 'Woof!'

That was his way of saying: 'What's the matter? Can I help you?'

'I wish you could, Tips,' said Mr Jonathan. And then he suddenly looked more cheerful. Perhaps Tips *could* help him. He looked round. The newspaper was on a chair, already tied up with string for Mrs Jones.

'There's the paper, Tips,' said Mr Jonathan, pointing. 'Fetch it here!'

Tips saw the paper, and took it into his mouth. He was just going to run off with it when Mr Jonathan called him back.

'Don't go yet, Tips,' he said. 'Bring the paper here.'

The clever little dog understood. He ran over to Mr Jonathan with the paper in his mouth. Mr Jonathan took a pencil from his pocket and wrote in large letters across the top of the paper:

'Mrs Jones. I have fallen off the ladder. Please fetch the doctor. Mr Jonathan.'

Then he pushed the paper once more into Tips's mouth and patted the waiting dog. 'Go home now,' he said.

Tips ran off, puzzling his little head to know why Mr Jonathan was on the floor. He ran to his mistress as soon as he reached Primrose Cottage and dropped the paper at her feet. She picked it up, and caught sight of the message scribbled on the top.

'Good gracious me!' she cried. 'Poor old Mr Jonathan! He's tumbled off the ladder!'

She ran for the doctor at once, and he took her along to Mr Jonathan's in his car. It wasn't long before they had him safely in bed, his leg bandaged up, and a nice hot drink beside him.

'It was my clever little dog Tips who found Mr Jonathan when he came for my weekly paper this evening,' said Mrs Jones proudly to the doctor. 'Mr Jonathan wrote a message on the paper, and, of course, I saw it when Tips dropped the paper at my feet.'

Mr Jonathan soon got well, and one morning Mrs Jones and Tips met him going shopping for the first time, leaning on a stick.

'Now wherever are you going?' cried Mrs Jones. 'I'm sure there's no shopping so important that I can't do it for you. Whatever is it you must buy, Mr Jonathan?'

'It's something very special,' said Mr Jonathan with a smile, and he went into a little shop nearby beckoning Tips and Mrs Jones in too. And what do you suppose the special bit of shopping was? Why, a fine red collar for Tips!

'That's to show everyone what a clever, helpful little chap he is,' said Mr Jonathan, putting it round the little dog's neck. 'He really does deserve it.'

I think so, too, don't you?

Mr Candle's Coconut

Mr Candle was very proud of himself. He had been to the Fair in Oak-Tree Village, and had won a coconut at the coconut shy. He had paid a penny to the man there, who had given him four balls to throw at the coconuts.

The first ball didn't go near any coconuts at all. It was a very bad shot. The second ball nearly touched the nut in the middle. The third ball went wrong somehow, and knocked off the hat of a man quite a long way away. After Mr Candle had said he was really very, very sorry, he took up his fourth and last ball, and threw that.

And, dear me, nobody was more surprised than he was to see it hit the very largest coconut of all and send it rolling to the ground! Mr Candle was simply delighted. He picked it up and took it home with him. All the way home he was making a fine plan.

He would give a Coconut Party. That would be a most unusual party. He would give his guests cocoa to drink, because that *sounded* as if it ought to go with coconut to eat. He would have a big coconut cake, some coconut ice candy and he would cut up the piece of coconut left and hand round the bits for his guests to nibble. Yes, it would be a very fine Coconut Party indeed.

So Mr Candle sent out his invitations. One went to Squiddle the Pixie. One went to Mrs Popoff the Balloon Woman, and the third one went to Mr Crinkle who painted wonderful pictures on the pavement outside the post office.

Mr Candle made his coconut cake. It was a beautiful one with coconut in it and grated cococut sprinkled on top. Then he made the coconut ice candy – some in pink and some in white. It tasted lovely because Mr Candle had a bit to see.

There was just over half the coconut left when Mr Candle had finished. So he cut this up very neatly into nice little squares, and put them on a plate on the wide window-ledge ready for when his guests came that afternoon.

When they came Mr Candle was ready to greet them, dressed up in his best green and red suit, with his new pointed shoes.

'Welcome to the Coconut Party!' he said. 'I am so pleased to see you. The party is because I won a coconut at the Fair.'

'How clever of you!' said Squiddle the Pixie.

'You *must* be a good shot!' said Mr Crinkle.

'Splendid, Mr Candle!' said Mrs Popoff, beaming all over her kind red face.

Mr Candle was so pleased. He thought what nice people his friends were. Down they sat to the coconut cake, the mugs of hot, sweet cocoa, and the coconut ice laid out on a blue dish. The pieces of coconut on the window-ledge were to be eaten after tea, when they were all playing games. It would be nice to have something to nibble at then, Mr Candle thought.

142

They finished all the coconut cake because it was so good, and they ate all the coconut ice candy too. They drank every drop of their sweet cocoa, and then they wanted to play games.

'Let's play Hunt-the-Thimble!' said Mrs Popoff, who simply loved that game. 'Mr Crinkle, you hide the thimble – here it is – and we'll all go out of the room while you do it.'

Out they went and shut the door. Mr Crinkle was a long time hiding the thimble. He simply could *not* think of a good place. But at last he put it on the head of a little china monkey on the mantelpiece. It looked just like a hat, and Mr Crinkle felt sure nobody would notice it was a thimble.

He called the others in, and they began to hunt. Mr Candle saw the thimble first and he sat down at once to show the others that he had seen it. He thought it would be a good idea to offer his friends a piece of the cut-up coconut on the window-ledge as soon as they had found the thimble too.

He got up to get the plate – and my goodness me, whatever do you think? There were hardly any pieces left! Somebody had taken them!

Who could it be? It must be Mr Crinkle. He had been a long, long time hiding the thimble when all the others were outside the door. Mr Candle was cross and upset.

'Did you eat my pieces of coconut?' he suddenly said to Mr Crinkle. 'There's hardly any left. You must have eaten them when you were supposed to be hiding the thimble.'

Mr Crinkle went very red.

'No, I didn't, Mr Candle,' he said, in a very hurt voice. 'I don't eat other people's bits of coconut unless they offer them to me. I hope I know my manners. I shan't stay and play with you any more. I shall go home.'

He put on his little red hat and walked out of the door. The others watched him go. Mr Candle felt very worried.

'He *must* have eaten the pieces of coconut,' said Squiddle the Pixie. 'He was the only one alone in the room.'

Suddenly there was a little noise at the window. Squiddle, Mr Candle and Mrs Popoff all turned round quickly. And what do you think they saw? I'll give you three guesses!

They saw three little birds there, blue-tits, dressed in pretty blue and yellow feathers – and they all picked up a piece of the white coconut and flew off out of the window in delight; for tits, as you know, love nuts, especially coconuts. I expect you have often hung up a coconut for them and watched them swinging upside down on it, pecking away as hard as they can.

'It's the tits!' cried Mr Candle. 'Look! The naughty little birds! They've taken away three more bits! They must have taken the other pieces too, but I expect Mr Crinkle was so busy trying to think of a good place to hide the thimble that he didn't notice the naughty little robbers.'

'I haven't found the thimble *yet*,' said Mrs Popoff, looking all round.

'How dreadful to tell Crinkle he had eaten the coconut when he hadn't!' said Squiddle the Pixie, looking worried. 'He was really very hurt about it.'

'I'll call him back and say I'm sorry,' said Mr Candle, shutting the window so that the blue-tits couldn't come in again. He ran to the door and looked up the street.

'Hi, Crinkle!' he shouted. 'Crinkle! Come back! You didn't eat the coconut — and we know who did.'

Mr Crinkle walked back, still looking rather cross and upset.

'It was the blue-tits who ate that coconut,' explained Mr Candle, taking his friend by the arm. 'Do forgive us for being horrid, Crinkle. There's just one piece left and you shall have that.'

Mr Crinkle was a very good-natured little

fellow, and he at once forgave Mr Candle and the others for saying he had done something he hadn't. He ate the last piece of coconut, and then said: 'What about a game of Blind Man's Buff?'

So they all played at Blind Man and had a lovely time together. And when they said good-bye Mr Crinkle said: 'I think a story ought to be written about how the blue-tits came and stole your coconut pieces, Mr Candle. Then it would warn people not to leave them near the window, if the blue-tits are about. Don't you think so?'

Mr Candle *did* think so – and that is why he told me to write this story!

Chipperdee's Scent

Once upon a time the Queen of Fairyland emptied her big scent-bottle, and asked the King for some new scent.

'I don't want any I've ever had before,' she said. 'Get me something strange and lovely, something quite different from anything I've ever had.'

So the King sent out his messengers all over the place – to the topmost clouds and to the lowest caves, begging anyone who knew of a strange and lovely scent to bring it to the

Queen. For reward he would give a palace set on a sunny hill, and twelve hard-working pixies to keep it beautiful.

Palaces were hard to get in those days, so anyone who had a lovely scent in bottle or jar journeyed to the Queen with it. But she didn't like any of them. She was really very hard to please.

Now there lived in a cave at the foot of a mountain a clever little pixie called Chipperdee. He spent all his days in making sweet perfumes, and he made them from the strangest things. And just about this time he finished making the strangest and loveliest perfume he had ever thought of.

He had taken twenty drops of clearest dew and imprisoned in them a beam of sunlight and a little starlight. He had taken the smell of the earth after rain and by his magic he had squeezed that into the bottle too. Then he had climbed up a rainbow and cut out a big piece of it. He heated this over a candle-flame and when it melted he let it drop into this bottle.

Then he asked a two-year-old baby to breathe her sweet breath into the full bottle – and lo and behold, the perfume was made! It smelt glorious – deep, delicious, and so sweet that whoever smelt it had to close his eyes for joy.

Now although he lived in a cave, the smell of this new perfume rose through the air and everyone who lived near smelt it. An old wizard sniffed it and thought: 'Aha! That is the scent that would please the Queen mightily! I will go and seek it.'

So off he went and soon arrived at the cave where Chipperdee sat working.

'Let me buy some of that new perfume of yours to take to the Queen,' said the wizard.

'No,' said Chipperdee. 'I am going to take it myself. I shall get a palace for it and twelve hard-working servants.'

'What do you want with a palace?' asked the

wizard. 'Why not let me give you a sack of gold for that bottle of scent? The Queen may not like it at all – and you will still have the sack of gold! I will not ask for it back.'

'You know perfectly well that the Queen will love this new perfume,' said Chipperdee. 'Go away, wizard. I don't like you, and you won't get any scent from me! I start tomorrow to journey to the Queen.'

The wizard scowled all over his ugly face and went away. But he made up his mind to follow Chipperdee and steal the scent from him if he could. So when he saw the pixie starting off, he made himself invisible and followed him closely all day long.

Chipperdee felt quite sure that he was being followed. He kept looking round but he could see no one at all. But he could hear someone breathing! It was very strange.

'It must be that wizard,' he thought to himself. 'He's made himself invisible. He's going to steal my bottle of scent when I sleep under a hedge tonight, Ho ho! *I'll* teach him to steal it!'

When it was dark the pixie found a nice sheltered dell. He felt all around until he found some little flowers with their heads almost hidden under heart-shaped leaves. He took out his bottle in the darkness, and emptied a little of the scent into each flower, whispering to them to hold it safely for him.

Then he filled the bottle with dew and set it beside him, curling up to go to sleep beneath a bush. He pretended to snore loudly, and almost at once he heard a rustling noise beside him, and felt a hand searching about his clothes.

The hand found the bottle and then Chipperdee heard quick footsteps going away. He sat up and grinned. Ho ho! The wizard thought he had got a fine bottle of scent – but all he had was a bottle of plain dew!

The pixie lay down again and slept soundly.

In the morning he woke up, and looked round at the little flowers near him. They were small purple flowers, so shy that they hid their heads beneath their leaves. The pixie jumped up and picked a bunch. He smelt them. Ah! His scent was in the flowers now, and it was really wonderful.

Off he went to the court, and there he saw the wizard just presenting the Queen with the bottle of plain dew that he had stolen from the pixie. How Chipperdee laughed when the Queen threw it to the ground and scolded the wizard for playing what she thought was a stupid trick on her!

The pixie stepped forward and told the Queen how the wizard had followed him and tried to steal his rare perfume. 'But, Your Majesty,' he said, 'I poured the scent into these little purple flowers, and if you will smell them, you will know whether or not you like the scent I have made.'

The Queen smelt the flowers – and when she sniffed up that deep, sweet, delicious scent she closed her eyes in joy.

'Yes!' she cried. 'I will have this scent for mine! Can you make me some, Chipperdee? Oh, you shall certainly have a palace set on a sunny hill and twelve hard-working servants to keep it for you! This is the loveliest perfume I have ever known.'

Chipperdee danced all the way back to his cave and there he made six bottles of the strange and lovely scent for the Queen. The King built him his palace on a sunny hill, and he went to live there with a little wife, and twelve hard-working servants to keep everything clean and shining.

But that isn't quite the end of the story – no, there is a little more to tell. *We* can smell Chipperdee's scent in the early springtime, for the little purple flowers he emptied his bottle into still smell of his rare and lovely perfume. Do you know what they are? Guess! Yes – violets! That's why they smell so beautiful – because Chipperdee once upon a time emptied the Queen's scent into their little purple hearts!

The Quarrelsome Tin Soldiers

Once upon a time there lived on a low wooden shelf two boxes of soldiers. One army was dressed in green and the other in red. The green army had horses to ride on, brown, black and white, but the red army had none. They carried guns, and the green horse-soldiers carried swords.

All the soldiers belonged to Kenneth. He liked them very much and often took them out to play games with him. He had a fine wooden fort, and he loved making his toy soldiers march up and down the drawbridge, and stand looking over the parapet of the fort.

The soldiers were very quarrelsome. The green horsemen hated the red foot-soldiers, and the red soldiers jeered at the green ones.

'You've only got stupid little swords,' said the captain of the red army to the green captain. 'We have fine guns. *You* wouldn't be much use against an enemy!'

'Ho, wouldn't we, then!' cried the green captain in a temper. 'Well, let me tell you this – *we* ride horses. *You* have to walk everywhere.'

'We don't mind that,' said the red captain, stoutly. 'We like marching. Anyway, it's silly to have horses you can't get off. You're stuck on to your horses, and even if you wanted to march you couldn't!'

Every night the two armies quarrelled and one night there was a battle. Kenneth's teddy-bear and a doll did their best to stop the fight, but it wasn't a bit of good.

'You'll only end in being broken to bits, said the doll. 'Then what will be the use of you? Kenneth won't want to play with you any more.'

'Hold your tongue, you stupid doll!' said the green captain, galloping over the doll's toes and making her yell. 'Now, men, follow me! We'll go to the toy fort and we won't let the red soldiers in. We'll keep them out and show them what poor fellows they are.'

All the horsemen followed their captain, and the green army galloped over the floor to the gay wooden fort. It was painted red and yellow and had four wooden towers and a drawbridge. Over the bridge galloped the soldiers and, as soon as they were in, one of them pulled up the drawbridge by its little chain. Now no one else could get into the fort, except by climbing up the walls.

The red soldiers had no horses so they could not go so fast as the green army. But they made haste and marched at top speed across the floor to the fort. By the time they reached it the green horse-soldiers were all in their places, looking over the top of the parapet, or cantering up and down the yard in the middle of the fort, shouting orders and feeling very important.

The red captain lined his men up in a row in front of the fort and told them to fire. Pop! Pop! Pop! The little guns went off and tiny bullets like seeds flew over the walls of the fort. Some of the green soldiers were hit and little holes were made in their tin uniforms.

They were very much upset. They shouted with rage, and galloped about, making quite a noise on the wooden floors of the fort. Then suddenly the green captain ordered the drawbridge to be let down and commanded six of his men to ride out and make a surprise attack on the enemy soldiers outside.

The red soldiers were so astonished that some of them were ridden down before they knew what was happening. One of them had an arm broken off and another one had his leg twisted the wrong way round. A third one lost his fine helmet, and cried bitterly because he couldn't find it.

'Courage, my men!' said the captain of the red soldiers when the green men had ridden back to the fort again. 'I am going to get the little cannon out of the nursery toy cupboard. With that we can shell down the walls of the fort, and rush in to attack the enemy.'

But the toy cannon was too heavy for the little tin soldiers to drag along. It shot peas, so it could have knocked over a great many of the green soldiers in the fort.

'Well, never mind if it's too heavy,' said the red captain. 'Look, we'll use a battering-ram instead. Here's one that will do.'

The battering-ram was really a big hoop-stick of Kenneth's. Seven soldiers picked it up and carried it to the fort. Then twelve red soldiers took hold of it, six on each side, and waited for their captain's word.

'Charge!' he cried, and fired off his little gun, making the doll nearly jump out of her skin, for she and the bear were almost asleep.

'Just look at those soldiers!' said the doll, sitting up. 'The

reds are breaking down one of the walls of the fort. Wouldn't Kenneth be cross if he knew!'

'Don't you think we ought to wake him?' said the bear anxiously. 'I think he would be very sorry if the tin soldiers killed one another. He would never be able to play with them again.'

'Let's go and wake him,' said the doll. So without telling the soldiers the two stole out of the day nursery into the night nursery, where Kenneth slept.

Bang! Bang! Bang! The hoop-stick battering-ram crashed against the wooden wall of the fort, and inside the green soldiers galloped about in a panic. What would they do if the wall gave way?

It did! It suddenly came away from the nails that held it and fell right down in the fort, knocking over two of the green soldiers as it fell. Then in poured the red soldiers, shouting in victory, shooting with their guns as they came.

The green soldiers soon pulled themselves together and they galloped at the enemy, slashing about with their swords, and that was how Kenneth found them when he came into the nursery with Doll and Teddy. He stood and stared in astonishment at his toy soldiers fighting one another so fiercely, slashing and shooting and yelling.

'How dare you behave like this!' he said suddenly. 'You will end in being broken to bits, and I didn't buy you to fight one another. I bought you to play with! Go back to your boxes and tomorrow I will come and talk to you.'

The soldiers had stopped fighting as soon as they heard Kenneth's voice. They were frightened. They trooped out of the wooden fort and went silently back to their boxes – all but seven of them who were so battered that they couldn't march or gallop.

The next day Kenneth lifted up the lids and looked at his toy soldiers. What a sight they were! Not one of them was whole.

'You're not fit to play soldiers with,' he said. '*You* haven't any arms – and *you* have only one leg – and *you* haven't a helmet – and *you* have a horse that has lost its head. What a dreadful sight you all are! I don't want you for soldiers any more. I shall have you for something else.'

So he took three of them for his railway station and made them porters. Four more he put on his toy farm to look after the hens and the sheep. Five of them he put to live in the dolls' house, and one of them had to drive the little toy motor-car. The others he thought would do to act in his toy theatre. Then he threw the cardboard boxes into the waste-paper basket, emptied out his money-box and went out of the nursery.

He bought a great big box of cowboys, some with horses and some without. How the soldiers envied them when they saw Kenneth playing games with them!

'You shouldn't have been so quarrelsome!' said the doll. 'It's your own fault that you're stuck away in the farm and the dolls' house, instead of being proper soldiers.'

'We wish we could have another chance!'

said the red and the green soldiers, looking longingly at the cowboys prancing about the floor on their big horses. But it wasn't any use wishing. They never did have another chance!

The Tall Pink Vase

Jill and Leslie lived in one of two cottages. The cottages were joined on to one another. One was called Buttercup Cottage and the other was called Daisy Cottage. Jill and Leslie lived in Buttercup Cottage, but Daisy Cottage was empty.

Then one day a furniture van arrived outside Daisy Cottage. The children were very much excited. Hurrah! Someone was coming to live in Daisy Cottage at last!

'I wonder what the people will be like,' said Jill. 'I do hope there will be some children.'

But what a disappointment! There were no children at all. Only a plump little lady with merry, twinkling eyes called Miss Bustle.

'Bother!' said Jill. 'I wish there had been a boy or a girl too.'

'Look at that dreadful pink vase going in,' said Leslie suddenly. 'Oh, Jill! Isn't it an ugly thing!'

Jill looked. It certainly was the ugliest vase she had ever seen. It was a bright pink, very tall and narrow, and had big yellow flowers here and there.

Jill's mother loved flowers and had many lovely vases – green jars, blue bowls and yellow jugs, which the children loved. They had never seen such an ugly thing as the pink vase going into the cottage next door.

'I don't think we shall like that person much if her things are all like that dreadful vase,' said Jill. 'I expect she will have paper flowers instead of real ones, and a china dog instead of a real puppy.'

'And mats that mustn't be dirtied, and cushions you mustn't lean against,' said Leslie. 'I don't think we'll make friends with our new neighbour, Jill.'

'Children, children!' called Mother. 'It's not polite to stare like that. Come away from the wall and play in the garden at the back.'

The children didn't bother any more about Miss Bustle. They went to school, played in the garden, went for walks and took no notice of the cottage next door at all. If they had, they would have seen that Miss Bustle was simply longing to smile at them and talk to them. But they ran by Daisy Cottage without a single look.

Then one day Leslie happened to look at Daisy Cottage from their back garden and he saw the dreadful pink vase standing at one of the windows.

'Oh, Jill, look! There's that ugly vase again!' he cried.

'Well, I *shan't* look,' said Jill. 'It was quite bad enough the first time. Come on, Leslie, let's play cricket with your new ball.'

'You can bat first,' said Leslie. 'I'll bowl.'

He bowled his new ball to Jill. She missed it and it went into the rose-bed. She found it and sent it back to Leslie. He bowled again.

It was an easy ball. Jill lifted her bat and swiped at it. Crack! She sent the ball right up into the air, spinning over the wall next door in the direction of the upstairs windows. The children watched it in fright. Would it break a window?

No – it struck the tall pink vase that stood at an open window and broke it in half! Crash! The pieces fell down inside the window. The cricket-ball rolled along the window-ledge and fell outside the window down to the flower-bed below.

The children looked at one another in dismay. Whatever would Miss Bustle say? They waited

for her to put her head out of the window – but nothing happened.

'Perhaps she's out,' said Leslie.

'Yes, I remember now – she is,' said Jill. 'I saw her go out with a basket about half an hour ago.'

'Let's go and get our ball,' said Leslie. So they climbed quickly over the wall, found their ball and climbed back. They sat down on the grass and looked at one another.

They were both thinking the same thing. If Miss Bustle was out, perhaps they needn't own up to breaking the vase. She might think the curtain had blown against it and knocked it down.

'Do you think we need say anything?' asked Jill at last.

Leslie went red. 'We *needn't*,' he said. 'But we must, Jill. We'd be cowards not to own up.'

'And, oh, dear, I expect Miss Bustle loves that vase better than anything in the world,' said Jill, with a groan. 'And we'll have to buy another out of our money-box.'

'Look, there she is, coming back,' said Leslie. 'Come on, Jill, let's get it over while we feel brave.'

So they went to the door of Daisy Cottage

and knocked. Miss Bustle opened the door and stared at them in surprise.

'Please,' said Leslie. 'we've come to say we're very very sorry but our cricket-ball broke your pink vase and if you'll tell us how much it was we'll buy you another.'

'Broken that pink vase!' exclaimed Miss Bustle. 'Have you *really*?'

'I'm afraid so,' said Jill, very red in the face.

'Well, I *am* glad it's broken at last!' said Miss Bustle, in a delighted voice. 'An old friend gave it to me and I've always hated it, but I didn't like to throw it away as it was given to me. I've always hoped it would get broken, it was so very ugly, but somehow it never did. And now at last it's smashed. Oh, dear me, I *am* glad! Come in, do, and have a bun and some lemonade, and see my new puppy. I only brought him home today.'

Well, would you believe it! Jill and Leslie were so surprised and delighted to hear that

Miss Bustle, instead of being angry with them, was really pleased! They could hardly believe their ears. They stepped inside and found that Daisy Cottage was the gayest, prettiest, cosiest little place they had ever seen.

She showed them the puppy in his basket and then went to get the lemonade and buns.

'Isn't it a pretty house?' said Jill to Leslie. 'Not a bit like we imagined. And isn't Miss Bustle nice?'

'You know,' said Miss Bustle, hurrying back with a jug, 'I didn't think you were very nice children. You never spoke to me or smiled. I thought you were horrid. But now I know better. It was so nice of you to come and own up about the vase, because it *might* have been one I liked. And I can see now that you are nice, bright, smiley children.'

Jill told Miss Bustle how they had seen the pink vase and hated it. 'We *were* silly!' she said. 'We thought you'd be like that vase, so we didn't bother about being good neighbours at all. Do forgive us.'

'Of course, of course,' said Miss Bustle, setting ginger buns in front of them. 'I'd forgive anyone anything if they had broken that horrid pink vase. Do come and see me often. I've got a nephew and niece coming to stay with me soon, so perhaps you would come out for picnics and motor rides with us?'

'Oh, *rather*!' said Jill and Leslie happily. 'Thank you very much!'

Now they are so much in Daisy Cottage with Miss Bustle and the puppy that their mother says she really thinks they ought to live there altogether!

'Wasn't it a good thing we owned up about that broken vase!' Jill often says to Leslie. 'We *should* have missed a lot of fun if we hadn't!'

Whiskers and the Parrot

Whiskers the cat lived with Miss Nellie, and was her great pet. He had a special chair of his own with a special cushion, a china dish with kittens all round it, and a saucer of blue and yellow.

So you can guess that he thought a great deal of himself. The other cats he met out in the garden didn't like Whiskers at all. They thought he was selfish, proud and stuck-up.

'One day you'll have your punishment,' said Tailer, the next-door tabby. But Whiskers yawned in his face very rudely and didn't even bother to answer.

And then Miss Nellie bought a parrot in a cage! Good gracious me, you should have seen Whiskers's face when he saw the parrot sitting in its cage in a sunny corner of the dining-room. The cage hung from a hook in the ceiling, and the parrot sat in the sun and fluffed out all her feathers.

She saw Whiskers and cocked her grey and red head on one side.

'Hallo, hallo, hallo!' she said.

Whiskers nearly shot out of the room with fright. What was this thing that looked like a big bird and talked like a human being?

'Woof, woof, woof!' said the parrot, pretending to bark like a dog.

Whiskers mewed in fright and ran under the table. He thought there really was a dog in the room.

'Ha-ha, ha-ha, ha-ha!' jeered the parrot.

'Hallo, hallo! Pretty Polly, pretty Polly!'

Just then Miss Nellie came into the room and laughed to see Whiskers under the table.

'Why, Whiskers!' she cried. 'Surely you are not frightened of my Polly parrot? I want you to be friends.'

But that was just what Whiskers was not going to be! As soon as he was used to the parrot and knew that it was only a big bird that could talk, he made up his mind to catch Polly somehow. He would wait until Miss Nellie was safely out of the way and then he would get down that big cage and eat the parrot.

So he waited his time, and at last his chance came. Miss Nellie went out to tea with a friend and left her parrot and her cat shut up in the dining-room together.

'Miaow!' said Whiskers fiercely, looking up at the cage. 'Now I'm going to get you!'

'Pretty Polly, pretty Polly!' cried the parrot,

climbing up and down her big cage. 'Hallo, hallo!'

Whiskers crouched to spring up at the cage. He leapt right up in the air and sprang on to the side of the cage. Crash – crash! The hook came out of the ceiling and the cage fell with a loud bang on to the floor!

Whiskers was frightened. He didn't know that his weight would bring the cage down. The parrot was frightened too. Whiskers ran into a corner to hide.

The parrot looked round – and saw that the crash had made the door of the cage fly open. Ha! Now she could get out and fly round a bit!

Out of the cage she hopped and flew up to the top of the curtain. Whiskers watched her in surprise. Perhaps he could get that parrot now. He crept out from the corner and lay watching, swishing his tail from side to side. The parrot saw the moving tail and suddenly flew down to the table. Before the surprised cat knew

what was happening the parrot shot down and nipped his tail hard, right at the tip.

'Miaow!' cried the cat in pain and surprise.

'Ha-ha, ha-ha!' laughed the parrot, sitting on the top of the clock. Whiskers leapt at the big bird, who at once spread her wings and flew to the electric light over the table, screeching loudly as she went. Then it was the parrot's turn. She suddenly flew at Whiskers and pecked him on the nose!

'Miaow!' wailed the cat, and the parrot flew up to the top of a picture, where she screeched and squawked very happily.

Whiskers wondered what to do. Then he thought of a good idea. He would creep into the parrot's cage and lie down there. Perhaps when it was dark the parrot would go back to her cage again and then Whiskers could get her! So as soon as the parrot's back was turned, Whiskers crept into the cage. Polly was happily pulling all the flowers out of a vase and took no notice of Whiskers at all.

Then she looked round to see where the cat was, and when she spied him in the cage how she laughed! In a trice the parrot flew down and shut the door of the cage with a clang. Whiskers was a prisoner!

'Ha-ha, ha-ha!' chuckled the mischievous parrot in glee, and settled down on Whiskers's own cushion, in Whiskers's own chair. Soon

Whiskers saw that the parrot was pulling all the fluff out of the cushion!

Whiskers mewed angrily and tried to get out of the cage – but the door was fast shut. Whiskers clawed at the door, but it was no good. He could *not* open it!

And there Miss Nellie found him when she arrived home again. The first thing she saw when she switched on the light was the parrot fast asleep on the curtain-rod. Then she saw the cage on the floor, and to her great surprise, spied Whiskers inside, with the door fast shut!

'O-ho, Whiskers!' she cried. 'So you jumped at the cage and made it fall down, did you? And Polly escaped out of the cage and you got in! And somehow or other the door was shut and made you a prisoner! Well, it serves you right. I shall leave you there for the night, and then, perhaps, you won't even *look* at the parrot-cage again.'

So there poor Whiskers had to stay all night

long, and Polly laughed and chuckled, screeched and squawked whenever she thought of him.

The next day the cage was opened and Whiskers crawled out. He ran into the garden, and found that all the cats there had heard what had happened – and how they teased him!

'You won't be so proud now, Whiskers!' they said. 'Who got caught in the parrot-cage? Ho-ho!'

And now Whiskers never takes any notice of the parrot at all, and would never dream of eating it – but Polly hasn't forgotten. She cries: 'Poor pussy, poor pussy!' whenever she sees Whiskers – and he doesn't like it at all!

The Odd Little Bird

Once upon a time there was a fine fat hen who was sitting on twelve eggs. Eleven of the eggs were brown but the twelfth was a funny greeny-grey colour. The hen didn't like it very much. She thought it must be a bad egg.

'Still,' she thought to herself, 'I'll see if it hatches out with the others. If it doesn't, well, it will show it is a bad egg.'

After many days the hen was sure her eggs were going to hatch.

'I can hear a little "cheep cheep" in one of

them!' she clucked excitedly to all the other hens. Sure enough one of the eggs cracked, and out came a fluffy yellow chick, who cuddled up in the mother-hen's feathers with a cheep of joy.

Then one by one all the other eggs cracked too, and tiny fluffy birds crept out – all except the greeny-grey egg. No chick came from that. It lay there in the nest unhatched.

'Well, I'll give it another day or two,' said the hen, sitting down on it again. 'After that I won't sit on it any more.'

In two days the hen found that the twelfth egg was cracking too. Out came a small bird – but it wasn't a bit like the other chicks!

It was yellow, certainly – but its beak was bigger and quite different. Its body was different too, and the little creature waddled about clumsily instead of running with the others.

The mother-hen didn't like it. She pecked

it and clucked: 'Oh, you funny-looking little thing! I'm sure you don't belong to me.'

The other chicks didn't like the little waddling bird, either. They called it names and shooed it away when it went to feed with them. It was sad and unhappy, for not even the mother-hen welcomed it or called it to enjoy a tit-bit as she did the others.

'I'm the odd one,' it said to itself. 'I wonder why? I can't run fast like the others, and I don't look like them either. I am ugly and nobody wants me.'

The odd little bird grew faster than the

others, and at last it was so much bigger that the little chicks didn't like to peck it any more, for they were afraid it might peck back and hurt them. So they left it alone, and stopped calling it names.

But the mother-hen was not afraid of it. She was often very cross with it indeed, especially when the rain came and made puddles all over the hen-run.

For then the odd little bird would cheep with delight and go splashing through the puddles in joy.

'You naughty, dirty little creature!' clucked the mother-hen. 'Come back at once. No chicken likes its feet to be wet. You must be mad, you naughty little thing!'

Then the odd little bird would be well pecked by the hen, and would sit all by itself in a corner, watching the rain come down and wishing it could go out in it.

One day it found a hole in the hen-run and

crept through it. Not far off it saw a piece of water, and on it were some lovely white birds, swimming about and making loud quacking noises. Something in the odd little bird's heart cried: 'Oh, if only I could be with those lovely birds, how happy I should be!'

But then it grew sad. 'No,' it said to itself, 'I am an odd little bird. Nobody wants me. But all the same I will just go to the edge of the water and paddle my feet in it. I can run away if those big white birds chase me.'

So off it went and paddled in the water. It was lovely. At first the big white ducks took no notice of the little bird, and then two came swimming up quite near to him.

'Hallo!' they cried. 'What a little beauty you are! Come along with us and have a swim. We'd be proud to have you.'

At first the little bird didn't know that the ducks were talking to him. But when he saw that they really were, he was too astonished to answer. At last he found his voice, and said: 'But, lovely creatures, surely you don't want me, such an odd, ugly little bird as I am!'

'You're not odd or ugly,' cried the ducks. 'You are a beautiful little duck, like us. Come along, it is time you learnt to swim. Don't go back to those funny little chicks any more. Live with us, and have a fine swim on the water!'

The odd little bird could hardly believe what he heard. So he wasn't odd or ugly, after all! He was only: different from the chicks because he was a duckling! And he would grow up to be like these lovely white creatures, and swim with them on the water. Oh, what happiness!

'Quack, quack!' he said, for the first time, and swam boldly out to join the ducks. The old mother-hen spied him through the hole in the run and squawked to him to come back. But he waggled his tail and laughed.

'No, no!' he cried. 'You will never make a hen of me. I'm a duck, a duck, a duck!'

The Meccano Motor-Car

Tom had made a Meccano motor-car to put Elizabeth's dolls in. It was rather a curious-looking car, but when Elizabeth had put in a few little cushions out of her dolls' house, and sat her dolls in the seat, it looked quite real.

'We shall have to push it along the floor because it won't go like a real car,' said Tom. 'Wait a minute though! Where's my clockwork engine? I know how to take the clockwork out of that, and perhaps I can put it into the Meccano motor-car.'

He tried it – and it worked! He wound up his home-made motor-car and it ran along the floor by itself, taking the dolls with it. Tom and Elizabeth were delighted.

They showed it to Mummy when she came to put them to bed.

'It's very good,' she said. 'Leave it there on the floor, and I'll show it to Daddy when he comes in.'

So they left it there, with all the dolls sitting on the seats. And that night, when everyone was asleep, you should have seen how excited those dolls were! They came alive and called to the sailor doll to wind up the Meccano motor-car to let it take them round and round the nursery again.

'I say!' said the curly-haired doll suddenly. 'Let's call the pixies in! They're holding a party under the lilac bush tonight, and they would so love to see our car.'

So they called to the pixies, and they all came

tumbling in at the window in great excitement.

'Let's have a ride, let's have a ride!' they cried, when they saw the motor-car. In they got, and one of the dolls showed them how to steer the little wheel. The pixies soon learnt how to drive, and my goodness me! how they tore about the nursery, almost running over the pink rabbit and nearly knocking down the blue teddy-bear.

They made such a noise that Tom and Elizabeth woke up. They slept in the room next to the nursery, and they sat up in bed and wondered whatever was happening.

'It sounds as if something was tearing about across the nursery floor,' said Tom. 'Whatever can it be?'

'Let's go and look!' said Elizabeth. So they crept out of bed and went to the day-nursery. The moon was shining right into it and they could see everything quite clearly.

And weren't they surprised! They saw their

toy motor-car tearing round and round, full of small pixies who were yelling with excitement. The dolls all stood watching, and the blue teddy-bear held up his paw, saying: 'Sh! Sh! Sh! Not so much noise! You'll wake the children!'

Tom and Elizabeth could hardly believe their eyes. They stood peeping in at the door, watching. And as they watched they saw the Meccano motor-car dash straight into a chair. Bump! It turned over and all the pixies fell out.

'Oh, my goodness!' cried Elizabeth, quite forgetting that she didn't mean to be seen.

As soon as she had cried out, all the pixies gave a squeal of fright and flew out of the window. The toys rushed back to the cupboard and sat themselves down at once, keeping as still as could be. The Meccano motor-car didn't move. It lay on its side.

Tom and Elizabeth were just going to step into the nursery when they heard their mother's voice.

'Elizabeth! Tom! Whatever are you doing? Go back to bed at once!'

'But, Mummy, such funny things have been happening in the nursery,' said Tom. 'We saw some fairies riding in the motor-car we made, and all the toys were alive!'

'Oh, nonsense! You were just dreaming,' said Mummy. 'Go back to bed before you get a cold, both of you!'

So to bed they had to go, and they soon fell

asleep again. In the morning they looked at one another.

'*Did* we really see those fairies and our toys all alive?' said Elizabeth. 'Or did we dream it?'

'Well, we couldn't *both* have dreamt it, could we?' said Tom. 'We'll see if the motor-car is still lying on its side in the nursery.'

It was! And do you know, tucked in one of the seats was a tiny silver wand with a shiny star on the end of it! One of the pixies must have left it behind.

'There!' said Elizabeth, in delight. 'It *was* real. We didn't dream it. Oh Tom! Let's use the wand and wish a wish!'

So when they are in bed tonight, they are going to wave that tiny wand and wish a wish. I do wonder what will happen!

The Jumping Frog

All the toys in the nursery were perfectly happy before the horrid jumping frog came. They used to play peacefully together, having a lovely time, never quarrelling, never snapping at one another or teasing.

But as soon as the jumping frog came he spoilt everything. For one thing he talked all the time, and for another thing he was always jumping out at the toys and giving them frights.

They couldn't bear him, but they were too polite to say so. They begged him not to frighten them, but he took no notice.

'You don't need to be frightened of *me*!' he would say. 'It's only my fun.'

But it wasn't fun to the toys. The teddy-bear fell over and bumped his nose when the frog jumped out at him from behind the cupboard; and the captain of the wooden soldiers broke his gun through tumbling down in fright when the frog jumped right on top of him.

'One of these days,' said the big humming-top solemnly to the frog, 'one of these days, frog, you will be sorry for all these tricks of yours. People who frighten others always end in getting a terrible fright themselves. And when that happens, *we* shan't help you!'

One night the jumping frog planned to frighten the doll. The frog could wind himself up, so he was able to jump about whenever he wanted to. He knew that the doll often walked round by the window at night so he thought he would hide behind the big waste-paper basket and jump out at her as she came walking by. How frightened the doll would be! How she would squeak! How fast she would run, and how the jumping frog would laugh!

The frog wound himself up and hid behind the waste-paper basket. He waited and he waited. At last he peeped out. Ah, was that the doll coming? Yes, it must be. Now for a good high jump to frighten her out of her skin!

The frog jumped – but oh, my goodness me! it wasn't the doll after all. It was the black kitchen cat! The jumping frog saw her just as he landed flat on the cat's back.

'Ssssssssssss-tt!' hissed the cat angrily, and flashed round to see what it was that had fallen on her back, and was now slipping to the floor. Out went her paw and gave the jumping frog a good smack. He leapt away in fright. The cat went after him.

All the toys peeped out of the cupboard in surprise. Whatever was happening?

'It's the frog!' cried the doll. 'He jumped out at the cat, thinking it was me, I expect. And now the cat is chasing him! Oh my, what a fright he is in.'

'Serve him right!' cried the toys.

'Help! Help!' squealed the frog, jumping for all he was worth.

But the toys were far too much afraid of the cat to go to his rescue. Each of them felt that the frog was getting what he deserved, and what he had so often given others – a good fright!

Jump! Jump! Jump! The frog leapt high in the air half a dozen times as the cat went after him. He was so frightened that he didn't look where he was going and once he nearly jumped right into the fire.

The toys watched, their eyes wide open in surprise. Whatever would happen?

Suddenly the cat shot her claws out at the frog and something clattered to the floor. It was the frog's key, which the cat had clawed out of his back. The frog jumped higher still, frightened almost out of his life. He was near the waste-paper basket, and to the toys' enormous surprise he jumped right into it!

He hadn't meant to — but there he was, at the bottom of the basket, among Nurse's bits of cotton and torn-up paper. And just at that very moment his clockwork ran down. He could jump no more. He couldn't wind himself up, either, because his key had fallen out. There he must stay.

The cat didn't know where the frog had gone. She hunted about for a while and then ran out of the nursery to catch mice in the kitchen. The toys ran to the waste-paper basket and peeped in.

'Help me out,' said the frog. 'I've had such a fright.'

'Serve you right!' said the doll sternly. 'We can't help you out, the basket is too tall. You'll be emptied into the dust-bin tomorrow, and that will be the end of you. You've always been fond of giving other people frights, so you can't complain of what has happened to *you*!'

The next morning the housemaid took the waste-paper basket downstairs, and emptied it into the dust-bin. The jumping frog went in all among the tea-leaves and potato-peel. He was very unhappy, and wished many times that he had been kind and jolly, instead of unkind and mean.

'I wonder what happened to him in the dustbin,' said the toys to one another. But no one ever knew!

The Little Brown Pony

Monty had a little brown pony for his birthday. It was a pretty little thing, not very tall, with a long brown mane and tail.

Monty wasn't very pleased. 'Pooh!' he said to himself when he saw it. 'Why didn't Dad give me a horse? I don't want a silly little pony! It won't be able to gallop nearly fast enough for me. I'd like a big horse that goes like the wind.'

He didn't say all this to his father, though. No, he didn't dare! His father called Monty to him and spoke gravely to him.

'Now listen, Monty,' he said. 'You are a very lucky boy to have a pony for your birthday, and I want you to be sure to treat it kindly and well. You are not very good with animals, for you let your rabbit die, and you never remembered to take your puppy for a walk when you had one. The gardener will teach you how to look after your pony properly, and you may ride him twice a day, if you wish. And remember, always be kind to him!'

Monty promised, but after a little while he grew bored with having to brush his pony and see to its water and food. He found that it couldn't go fast enough for him and soon he began to smack it and shout at it. The little thing was frightened and did its best for Monty, but he was impatient and unkind.

The small girl who lived next door to Monty often used to watch him riding the pony. She had always wanted a pony of her own, but her daddy couldn't afford one. So she watched

Monty's pony instead, and sometimes she would climb over the wall and go to help the gardener groom the pretty little animal.

'Do you like doing that sort of work?' asked Monty scornfully one day, watching Ann brush his pony till its coat gleamed and shone.

'Yes, I do,' said Ann. 'I wish I could do it always. I love your little pony, Monty.'

'Well, look here – if you'll look after my pony for me, I'll let your ride it once a week,' said Monty. 'I hate looking after it. It's a silly animal, anyway. I want a great big horse that will gallop!'

Ann promised to care for his pony each day, and once a week Monty let her have a short ride on it. Ann grew very fond of the pony, and the fonder she grew the more she hated seeing Monty whip the little animal and shout at it.

'You shouldn't do that,' she said to him. 'It's unkind.'

'Hold your tongue!' said Monty rudely.

'Whose pony is this, yours or mine? I shall do what I like with it!'

The pony grew frightened of Monty and one day when the boy galloped it round and round the field, slashing it with a big stick, the pony lost its temper. It stood quite still and wouldn't move a step. Ann was watching over the wall, and she shouted to Monty to jump off.

'Stop it, Monty!' she called. 'The pony is getting angry.'

'What do I care!' cried Monty, and he hit the pony hard. It suddenly galloped off, nearly throwing Monty, and rushed for the open gate that led into the road. Ann saw that it was running away with Monty. In a trice she was over the wall, and reached the gate just as the pony got there. She caught hold of the reins and dragged at them with all her strength.

The pony stopped just outside the gate, and Monty slid off. Ann's arms were almost pulled out of her shoulders.

'You're a cruel boy!' she said, through her tears. 'You don't deserve to be saved when the pony's running away. I wish *I* had him! I'd love him and be kind to him. You don't like him a bit. You don't even look after him. I do all that!'

'What's all this?' said a deep voice, and who should look over the hedge at the other side of the road but Monty's father. 'Ann, I saw what you did. You're a brave little girl, and I'm proud of you. As for Monty, I'm thoroughly ashamed of him. I saw him lashing the pony and I don't wonder it ran away.'

Monty's father led the pony back to its stable and there he heard from the gardener how Ann looked after it each day, and how all that Monty did was to ride it and whip it every day. Monty's father looked very stem. 'Very well,' he said to Monty. 'You have disobeyed me. Now you must be punished. As Ann loves the pony and looks after it so well, she shall have it for her own. You don't deserve to go riding at all, and you are never to ride the pony again. It's Ann's now.'

Well, what do you think of that? Ann was so overjoyed that she could hardly say a word. Monty turned red and ran off. The pony gave a little whinny of delight and snuggled its nose into the small girl's hand.

'I'm happy now!' whinnied the pony.

'So am I!' cried Ann. 'We'll have *lovely* times

together!' They do, too – you should just see them galloping round the field on a sunny morning! As for Monty, he always looks the other way.

About the Author

Enid Blyton, who died in 1968, is one of the most successful children's authors of all time. She wrote over seven hundred books, which have been translated into more than forty languages and have sold more than 400 million copies around the world. Enid Blyton's stories of magic, adventure and friendship continue to enchant children the world over. Her beloved works include The Famous Five, Malory Towers, The Faraway Tree and the Adventure series.

Enid Blyton

The Adventure series

Which ones have you read?